# The One Million Stories Creative Writing Project 2010 Anthology

Published in 2010 by The One Million Stories Creative Writing Project.

First Edition

Copyright © Text millionstories.net
The author asserts the moral right under the Copyright, Designs and patents Act 1988 to be identified as the author of this work.

All Rights reserved. No part of this publication may be reproduced, stored in a retrieval system, or transmitted, in any form or by any means without the prior written consent of the author, nor be otherwise circulated in any form of binding or cover other than that in which it is published and without a similar condition being imposed on the subsequent purchaser.

Published by
The One Million Stories Creative Writing Project.
All Rights Reserved. 2010.

ISBN 978-1-4467-0353-3

All works published in this collection remain the sole copyright of the credited authors and appear in this volume under licence to the One Million Stories Creative Writing Project.

Cover Design and Photograph © millionstories.net

# The One Million Stories Creative Writing Project

## 2010 Anthology

*Edited by*
*Simon Million*
*with thanks to the OMSCWP Team*

*Contents*

**Introduction**
*Simon Million... 7*


**A Short Primer on the Mechanics of Flight**
*Joe Miller...11*
**Eatin' Chicken**
*Jemma Hathaway...31*
**The Iron Plank**
*Muhammad Ashfaq...37*
**Dancefloor In Outer Space**
*Paul G. Duke...51*
**Glitch**
*Ed Wood...74*
**Lullaby: Barcarole**
*Ke Huang...81*
**The Country Club**
*J.F. Chavoor...95*
**Embroidering**
*Viccy Adams...103*
**Girl on a Street Corner**
*Vivienne McCulloch...111*
**Jam Tomorrow**
*Abi Wyatt...115*

**Apocalypso**
*John Rachel...121*
**A Drying Day**
*Vivienne McCulloch...129*
**Body Parts**
*Kathleen Doherty...137*
**Stella's Starwish**
*Erica Verrillo...153*
**Galileo's Hood**
*C.B. Heinemann...169*
**The Corridors of Power**
*Clare Glennon...183*
**Strike Up The Band**
*Virginia Moffatt...187*
**The Entrails**
*Muhammad Ashfaq...191*
**Time To Go**
*Simon Kellow-Bingham...201*
**Being Twenty One**
*J.F. Chavoor...207*

**About The Authors**
*...215*
**Reader's Comments on "The Iron Plank"...223**

# Introduction

**Welcome to the second volume** of short stories from the One Million Stories Creative Writing Project. This document presents twenty of the best submissions to the site throughout 2010. It has been a good year for stories, a good year for meeting new writers from all over the globe, and a good year for seeing regular contributors develop their writing voice.

We all love the thrill of opening up a new story fresh from the Internet to discover something original and 2010 saw many more than the year before. The collection reflects the contemporary feel to the submissions, referencing world-wide events almost as they happened.

This is exactly what the OMSCWP was set up to capture from the start, the global zeitgeist. We set out to find out what the world was thinking, the anti-fake world, the one we all live in. For many years readers have been sold what to think, sold what to feel, but this is a book full of the real thing. What links all of these stories and their authors is their very authenticity.

For this success we are grateful and immensely honoured to receive so many exciting stories from so many talented writers. You will, as a reader, be meeting these writers at different stages of their career; some are starting out into the world of letters, while others are more established in their writing. Some of these writers come to us from other walks of life altogether.

We read many other stories this year, many more than we expected, but read them all we did. It was not an easy task picking out the twenty stories for the anthology and there were disagreements and debates over coffee, tea, soup and sandwiches. What we are certain of now is that this collection is a robust and representative selection of excellent new writing crying out for new readers, and that is our mission.

A Million thanks,

*Simon Million*

*About the OMSCWP*: The Project was founded in 2008 during a road trip across Northern France by Simon Million. Its aims include, but are not limited to, the promotion of the short story form from fifty to five-thousand words, the promotion of excellent new writing from every continent on Earth, putting great fiction in front of deserving readers everywhere and rising above bedlam.


All of the authors can be contacted at
author@millionstories.net

# A Short Primer on the Mechanics of Flight

*Joe Miller*

It had been a tedious week. A tiring week. An enervating week.

Want to know what it's like training salesmen?

Apart from product knowledge, it involves making sure they don't let their briefcases fall open at the wrong moment, spilling their contents all over the customer's floor. You laugh, but you'd be surprised.

And smiling. Holding eye contact. A firm handshake. Speaking clearly. And, of course, knowing how to close the sale. Plenty of different methods. My favourite's the 'silent close'. That always weeds out the nervy ones. The ones who can't hack it. Won't make it.

We video the sessions. Make 'em sit down and analyse them. Do it again, and again, and again. Until they get it right. Then we give them a nice certificate saying they're fit for purpose.

Do it in my sleep these days.

Then we pack 'em off with good wishes and exhortations to maintain a positive mental attitude. PMA all the way. "You've got the stuff, alright." "Go kill, tiger." Yadda, yadda.

Bullshit.

They keep in with us because they know they'll be back in due course, for more of the same.

But, the final session ended. The day ended. The week ended. Thank God.

Going home.

Friday evening. Flight booked. A few hours and I'd be back in Edinburgh, meeting Ishbel and the rest of the gang.

The end of week gathering. I like Fridays.

I quite like Ishbel, too.

Coming home, baby.

Yeah.

The domestic departure lounge was full of people heading for various UK destinations.

Noisy here. Bar doing good business. Always does.

Laughter. Earnestness. Sincerity. Mendacity. Bit of hope here and there. Probably a bit of desperation, too.

Mainly business people. Self-important. Believers in their own propaganda.

Aren't we all?

Large gin. Not alone in that. Not by any means.

"Ladies and gentlemen, Flight BA 576 to London is subject to a slight delay. This is due to the incoming flight from Paris which is undertaking an emergency landing. However, we anticipate no difficulties and hope to be boarding very soon. If you could please bear with us. We apologise for the delay. There will be another announcement, shortly."

That concentrated our thinking. For a second or two.

Window.

"Is that it? That the Paris flight?"

"Think so."

There it is. Down you come, Chérie. That's it.

Fire engines rolling along, blue lights strobing off the wet tarmac. But it's safely on the deck. All's well, then.

Window clears of gawpers.

Another gin.

Get those London people away, can't you? Then I can get home. Weekends are short enough.

"Good evening, ladies and gentlemen. Flight BA 576 to London is now ready for boarding. Passengers for this flight should make their way to Departure Gate B. Please have your boarding cards ready."

Must have heard me.

Empties the place a bit, though there's some early arrivals wandering in for the next batch of flying zoos in an hour and a half's time.

"Ladies and gentlemen, Flight BA 582 to Edinburgh is now ready for..."

Hell's teeth, that was quick. Down remainder of gin. Bloody Gordon's. Bunch of bastards for reducing the proof strength. Never forgiven them for that.

Right then. Let's get this show on the road.

Coming home, baby.

Yeah.


Window.

Can't see much in the dark. Still raining. Plane hasn't moved yet. Guy next to me pulls his briefcase back out from under his seat. Tag on it. Director of a construction firm. Big bloke. Probably would have preferred the aisle seat. But there's a middle-aged woman in that with a 'don't disturb' look about her.

They've already done the emergency drill thing. Ignored as usual.

Sigh inwardly. What's the hold-up? Come on. I wanna get going. There's a book in my briefcase, but it's in the overhead. Stupid of me. Not much of a book, anyway. Come on, will you?

Heads up.

"Good evening, ladies and gentlemen. I'm your senior flight attendant on this British Airways flight to Edinburgh. My name is Monica ..." Sounds like Seles. But that can't be right. Unless she starts grunting. "I do apologise for the slight delay in departure, but we're being held here for the moment by Flight Control as the London plane which took off a short time ago has to return to the airport. We should be cleared for take-off as soon as it touches down."

And that's it. Short and sweet, Monica.

Another emergency landing? Bet the London lot are chuffed. Busy night for the airport fire brigade, too. But that's what they signed up for.

Glance at the big bloke on my right. Raise my eyebrows. He gives a short, dismissive smile. Returns to his documents.

Window.

Still dark. Still raining.

Come on.

Ah.

"Ladies and gentlemen, we have now been cleared for take-off. Please ensure your seatbelts are fastened, your seats are in the upright position and any hand luggage not secured in the overhead lockers is stored safely beneath your seat. I would remind you that smoking is strictly forbidden and..."

Yeah, yeah. Gerronwithit.

"The cabin lights will now be dimmed though you can continue to use the reading light which you will find above your head."

And we start to roll towards the main runway as the attendants walk up and down the aisle, checking to see we've obeyed their instructions like the good little sheep we are.

No messing about this time. Looks like they've given the pilot a short window of opportunity and, almost as soon as we line up, we're accelerating down the strip.

Always like this bit. Bit of brute speed.

And we're off. Climbing steeply into the sky.

Climbing.

Big cigar tube at three hundred miles an hour and rising. Seems daft, somehow.

Climbing.

Still climbing.

And that's when it happens.

That's when the alarm goes off in my head.

*Something wrong with this plane* yells the organism. *Get off this plane. Now!*

What?

*Don't like this. Not good.*

Whaddayamean, there's something wrong with the plane?

*Something wrong! Something wrong!*

What? What are you telling me, for Christ's sake?

Still climbing.

Hair really does rise on the nape of my neck. First time for everything.

*Something wrong. Something wrong.*
I glance around me. Unnerved. But can't detect anything out of sorts. No one else seems bothered.
Nothing.
Plane starting to level off.
*I'm telling you, there's something not right.*
I can't see anything!
*Get off the plane.*
Don't be so fucking stupid.
*I'm telling you!*
Well, what? What! I can't see anything wrong.
*Listen...*
No. You listen. That's enough. Going rational. Ignoring you. So shaddap and give me peace.
*I'm telling y...*
Plane levels off.
And the voice in my head recedes as I override it.
What was that all about?
Take a deep breath. Sit back in my seat. The seatbelt light goes off.
Construction man is back in his paperwork.
Drinks trolley'll be down soon. Hear them preparing it.
Another gin and everything'll be fine. Bit more tired than I thought is all. That and too rich an imagination.
Voice in my head almost mute, now. Home soon.
Coming home, baby.
Yeah.
Here comes the trolley.
Great.
Gin.
Then it doesn't.
They wheel it back. Sharpish.
Seatbelt light comes back on.

Then:

"Attention. Attention. This is an emergency announcement. It is essential you pay attention. This is an emergency announcement."

What?

*Told you so. Told you so. Told you so.*

Construction man is clutching his papers. Mrs 'don't disturb' is clutching her armrests. She's disturbed now.

This is not good. Not good.

Neurons fire up, adrenaline pours into system, pulse rate rises, breathing faster now, blood vessels dilate. Fight or flight. But there's no one to fight and I'm stuck on this bloody flight. Shit.

*Told you so.*

Bugger off. Need to focus.

*Just trying to help. It's my job.*

Shut the fuck up!

"The pilot has detected a malfunction and we are returning to Birmingham immediately. It is essential you pay attention to this announcement and follow our instructions precisely."

Christ. We're already descending fast. I mean, we're not falling out of the sky, but we're losing height hellish quickly. Can passenger planes do this?

It's gone very quiet.

I go somewhere else. Perhaps it's panic. It feels like panic. But I don't have much experience. Is this it? Am I going to die? I think maybe I am and it's a very bad feeling.

Been in a few dodgy car shunts and the like. And once, in Spain, had to run like buggery from a gang of yobs with knives. None of that was fun but nothing like this. Having trouble breathing. No control over events. Not good at that. Remember a story about a

Japanese plane that crashed into a mountain. All dead. Passengers wrote letters to their families as they went down. Gutsy lot. Should I do that? Write notes to my kids?

Divorced with two children. Didn't tell you that before. Now you know.

It doesn't occur to me to write to Ishbel.

Seem to come back from wherever I was. Not so quiet in here now. Someone cries out. Not a scream, but like a low howl. Someone else is weeping. And I can hear retching further back.

Monica's still going. Voice tight. How long was I away for? Not long, obviously.

"...and make sure everything loose is stored securely in the back of the seats in front of you. Any hand luggage not in the overhead lockers must be secured as tightly as possible beneath your seats. If you have removed, or loosened shoes, then please replace them and make sure they are firmly on your feet. If any mobile phones are switched on, you must switch them off now. Bring your seats to the upright position. If the oxygen masks are released..."

Her wound-up voice continues.

But, we're still in the air. And, from somewhere, somewhere, I manage to find a degree of self-control. As if some other, stubborn little part of the organism has made itself known to me, and is *not* prepared to let me roll over in the face of something as minor as a potentially fatal plane crash.

Touch and go there for a minute, though.

What're the odds of three emergency landings in a row?

But my God, we're still going down fast. Pilot's in one hell of a hurry. Aren't we supposed to circle round and jettison fuel or something?

Got to do something. What can I do? Look around.
Next to me, construction man is ashen-faced. Heard the term before, but never actually seen it. He's rigid. Gripping the armrest as if he's trying to choke it. Right hand holding a photograph of a girl in front of him. Staring at it. Hand shaking. Looks a bit young for a wife. Maybe a daughter. Maybe not.

I put my right hand over his left arm. Give it a squeeze.

"We're going to be okay," I say.

He looks round. Tries to move his face muscles. Can't. Manages a sort of grimace, finally. Nods. Can't speak.

"We'll be fine," I add. Remove my hand. Hope it helped him.

Not much else I can do.

Hate this helplessness. Feel rage. Control it.

"...as the plane lands, you must lean forward with your head to your knees and clasp your hands firmly behind your head. When it is time to do this, we will announce, brace, brace, brace. I repeat, we will tell you, brace, brace, brace. Now, please ensure your seatbelts are firmly fastened."

Quite serious this, then.

But for some reason, I think we might make it. I think. Maybe.

Stewardesses come down the aisle, struggling to keep their balance as the plane angles down, checking everybody, trying to reassure, but they look so bloody scared themselves it's not much help.

Not like the practice sessions you did, eh, girls?

Window.

There's the ruddy airport. Must be one of the fastest controlled descents in history. Jesus, can we land at this speed?

Looks like we're going to try, anyway.

"Brace. Brace. Brace."

Bugger that.

If this thing's going to fall apart or burst into flames, I want to see what's going on. Be ready for whatever it is I'm going to try and do. Not going out with a whimper. Bloody not, I tell you.

Check the location of the emergency exits.

Weird, looking around. Everyone else's heads are below the tops of their seats.

Window.

And we're down. Bump into the air, twice, then down again. And we're on the ground. God, we're shifting. Apply the bloody brakes will you?

Fire engines racing alongside us, falling behind, and then catching up as we slow. Busy night for you then, lads.

And we roll to a stop. Isolated. Away from the terminal. Surrounded by red fire trucks with flashing blue lights and large nozzles aimed directly at us.

Seatbelt already unbuckled, I'm thinking emergency chutes. But, apparently not.

"Ladies and gentlemen, please remain in your seats with your seatbelts fastened."

A lot of chatter, now. Someone's still weeping. Construction man has put the photograph away but he's still on the pale side of chalk.

*Told you so.*

So how was I supposed to get off the bloody plane, then?

*My job's to warn you what you need to do, not tell you how to do it.*

Yeah, right. Fine. You did it. Thanks.

*You're welcome.*

You can go, now.

Window.

Still raining. A set of steps are rolled up to the leading exit door. Men in heavy duty clothing come aboard. Enter the cockpit.

Some come out.

They go back in.

They all come out.

We sit.

Three airport buses appear alongside.

"Ladies and gentlemen, we will be disembarking you from the rear exit of the plane. Buses will transport you to the terminal where representatives will meet you to organise onward travel arrangements."

I'm waiting for her to say thank you for flying British Airways. But she doesn't. Probably best.

The seatbelt lights go out.

Coming home, baby.

Yeah.

Bloody hope so, anyway.

They've laid on a plane for us. Another incoming flight from Paris. Ironic. Should have stopped here. But they're sending it on up to Edinburgh.

Half the passengers have taken the train vouchers and buggered off. Understandable I guess.

The rest took the free meal and the offer of another flight. Construction man's still with us. I'm surprised. Like getting back on a horse, I suppose.

I reckoned lightning wouldn't strike twice when I accepted.

Then I thought about three emergency landings in a row.

Stuff it. Wanted to get home tonight.

Apparently, our plane suffered an electrical fire in the cockpit.

Had to try and get the thing down again rather quickly as they weren't quite sure what systems were working and what ones weren't. No time for a fuel dump.

Great.

Managed to get hold of Ishbel on the phone. Explained. Reckoned I'd be there before closing time. They'd all wait.

Nice girl, Ishy. Been together three years now. Don't live with her. Bit leery of that. But it's always her place on a Friday night.

Runs her own dress shop. Dress designer. Successful. Breaking in her senior assistant to take more time off. Getting broody. We don't talk about that. But it's there. Lurking in the background.

Quite a lot lurking in the background, really.

"Good evening, ladies and gentlemen..."

Here we go again, then.


Drinks trolley's busy. Hardly surprising.

Everyone necking large ones.

"Something else, sir?"

They know we've had a bit of an evening of it.

Construction man's further up the aisle. 'Don't disturb' must have taken the train.

Place is half-empty. I've got three seats to myself. Window.

Clear night here. Darker ahead.

There goes Newcastle, glinting far below.

And we're over the border.

Coming home, baby.

I chuck some peanuts down my throat and wash them down with more booze.

And the seatbelt lights come on.

Bit early for that isn't it?

"Good evening, ladies and gentlemen. You will notice that the seatbelt sign is on. Would you please restore your trays to the back of the seat in front of you and bring your seats to the upright position."

What?

"We may be about to experience a little turbulence on our approach to Edinburgh due to weather conditions, but there is nothing to be alarmed about."

Oh for God's sake.

And this plane too, goes quiet as the stewardesses collect our plastic tumblers, our empty miniature bottles, our peanut packets and our anxious looks.

The Pentland Hills guard the southern approaches to Edinburgh and the thunder storm which rolls around their summits is confined to the locality.

But it does not prevent the plane jerking haphazardly around the sky in ways, one assumes, pilots are taught specifically to avoid. Bad for business.

Window.

Forget the window.

Just get us down.

At least the organism's keeping quiet this time, so I guess we're probably going to make it.

Only a bloody thunder storm. Lousy timing though.

And we get out of it and descend over the Forth and glide across Cramond, annoying its snotty residents with our jetty noise, and we land. We land.

And it feels good.

No one's smiling as we exit. We just want off.

Raining again.

No room at docking as, I guess, it's an unscheduled flight. So we walk across a short stretch of glistening, reflective tarmac to the terminal building.

Relief still washing through me like a purge.

And as we walk, I overhear one orange-jacketed airport worker say to another: "They look like that lot that got off that flight back in..."

But I don't hear the rest.

Just want to get to my car and get out of here.

I like my wheels. Comforting. Familiar. *Grounded.*

Work for a blue chip company. Prestigious name. Money's good. Do well and you're rewarded well. Job's a bore but so what? Do better and you're promoted. And they give you nicer wheels. Lines of least resistance. Easy. Don't think about it too much.

Shouldn't be driving. Know that.

Don't care. Not tonight.

Need to get away. Get to the pub and tell my story. Centre of attention. Bask in concern. See Ishy. Feel her arms around me. Her sometimes predatory lips. The future's for another day. Isn't it?

Coming home, baby.

Yeah.

Window.

Pay the ticket. Nothing behind me. Pull out.

And into the city.

Watch it, now. Take it easy. Stick to the limit. Use the indicators.

It'll be fine. Look what I've just come through.

Through Corstorphine, past the Zoo, sharp left at Ellersly Road then up and along Ravelston Dykes, down to Queensferry Road, right for a bit then left towards Stockbridge. Through St Bernard's Crescent – got divorced from that house there; should have hung on to it – and right at the end of Leslie Place, over the Water of Leith and stop at the lights.

Sense of direction's still there, then.  And my driving's okay. Mustn't attract attention.

Green.

Car in front pulls away. And stalls.

And I hit the back of it.

Shit. Shit. Shit.

Me to blame. No question in law.

I work for a professional company.  And a tough one. Lose your licence, lose your job.

Shit.

Think.

*Bluff it.*

Was going to do that, anyway.  Don't always need your help.

Silence. Maybe *it's* sulking.

Get out. Superficial damage.

Walk up to driver's window of other car.  Still raining.

She lowers her window, looks out.

"Lishen, it'sh..."

"What the hell do you think you were doing?" I say angrily, while my brain's interpreting, fast.

"Lishen, it'sh all my fault. Shtalled it. Me."

She's a lot more pissed than I am.  Another woman in the passenger seat.

I look doubtful.

"Really shorry," she says.

"Tell you what," I say. Mr Beneficent. "There's not much damage. I'll let it go this time. Save bothering with our insurance companies. Okay with that?"

"Yeah. Absholutely. Thanksh, mishter. Thanksh."

And she manages to get it started and into first, and drives off.

I do the same.
Heart pumping a bit. Close one, that.
How much more crap do I need tonight?
Get out of here, now. Fast.
And I do. Swing left.
Through the centre's cobbled streets and, eventually, into Albany Street. Park. Lock it. That won't move again tonight. Pocket keys.
Cross the street and through the welcoming doors to a cheer from the big corner table.
"Yay."
"Here he is."
"You made it."
"Yeah."
And Ishy's lips are on mine and there's a pint in my hand and all's well.
Except it's not. And I don't know why. It's just that there's this thing at the back of my mind, like a stone in a shoe, that wasn't there earlier but has somehow slipped in between the leather and the sock.
When you're plummeting through the sky at four thousand feet a minute or whatever it was, a lot of stuff crosses your mind.
Fuck it.
Consign.
It can wait.
I'm home, baby.
Yeah.

Adrenaline's a powerful drug.
Coming down, now.
She'd been quite voracious in a wet, slightly drunk kind of way, had Ishy. I hadn't really been up for it but there hadn't been a lot of choice in the matter.

She seemed to have enjoyed it, anyway. Now she was dozing off. Snoring gently, purring really. Mouth hanging open. Not the best of looks.

Her head was tucked into my left shoulder and her left arm stretched across my chest and up to my other shoulder. My left arm was down her back. Nowhere else for it to go.

You'd think I would have been ready to sleep for a week.

Anything but.

Still reliving that bloody take-off and landing. Couldn't get the first emergency announcement out of my head.

Interesting that that before it all went tits up, I seemed to *know* there was something wrong with that plane even though I didn't know what. Like extra-sensory perception. Wonder if that's not so much something evolutionary we've yet to acquire, but something we've lost? Makes more sense to me when I think about it.

Thoughts jumping round my head like fleas on heat.

'Wound my heart with monotonous languor.'

Where the hell did that come from?

Some old movie, I reckoned.

Like I said, a nice girl, Ishbel. Girl? Woman, I mean. Thirty-three to my thirty-five. But I've got two kids and I don't want any more. Nor another wife.

Must remember I'm seeing my BUs (biological units I call them, for a laugh) on Sunday. My time for them. Only ever at weekends. Try and think of something interesting for them to do for a change, otherwise they'll just sit around my place watching television and bickering and wanting things for tea that I haven't thought to get in. Better phone Lizzie tomorrow – that's the ex – and make sure I have the time right to pick them up. Pisses her off when I'm late. Which is fair enough.

Boss man, Ken, says I'm in line for a promotional move to head office. But do I want it? Effing North London. Lovely. And that'll be me. Clawing up the greasy pole for the rest of my life. Not as if I enjoy what I do. It's just...what? Easier? Avoidance?

Not going to go. I know it now. Only really realised that today. Shit. What's that going to mean?

Arm's a bit stiff. But Ishbel's turned into a log. A small log with long, jet black curling hair and a pale, almost alabaster skinned body. Getting slightly pudgy these days. Just a little. Sign of things to come.

Going to have to sort this out with her. Not fair otherwise. She's thinking kids. Every time she sees a baby in a bloody pushchair she smiles and squeezes my arm. Hasn't said it outright, but I can hear that train coming down the tracks. Heading for me. And I don't want it. Time for flight. Christ. How many ruddy life-changing decisions am I about to have to make?

No. Got to do the right thing. For her. Yeah, okay, and me. Get out before it's too late. Be decent.

Don't understand it. Everything seemed fine. Now I feel like...like I was perfectly safe in my chrysalis, but the skin's cracked open and I can't seal it shut again. Don't like this.

Ishy's parents took us out once. They'd been pushing to meet me. Took us to a dinner dance. Didn't know such things still existed. Some god-awful throwback of a place near Stirling. Even had ham and pineapple on the menu. And the guys in the band had these little short blue jackets with braid on them. Like going out to an archive.

One and only time I met them. They thought I was a good thing. That's charm and salesmanship for you.

Window.

Her flat's on the top floor of a Victorian block. Bed's on a raised floor on one side of the bedroom. There's a big skylight window above it. Four panes of glass wide, by five deep. It's what appealed to her about the place. You can lie here and watch the sky. Bit of light pollution from the city at night, but it's still quite something.

Kimonos hanging around the walls. She collects them. Low shelves with her books of lightweight philosophy and volumes of popular poetry. Lot of glass and Indian bronze.

Nice room, though. Safe. Comforting. Or it was.

I suppose I can just lie here and let my arm go numb rather than disturb her. Least I can do.

Window.

Night's clear again. Watch stars. All that ancient light.

Light a cigarette, one handed. Lie smoking in the orangey dark.

Sirens in the background. Edinburgh city centre late on a Friday night. Like the Russians storming Berlin. You don't want to be out there.

There are many kinds of certainty in this life. But I don't like the ones settling in my mind right now. There's an inexorability to them. As if I have no choice. Or, at least, no *worthy* choice. Fuck. How is this happening? I was fine this morning.

But it *is* happening.

Shit.

Try and shove my thoughts away. But they continue to settle, like absolutes.

Thirty thousand feet above me, up there in the deep midnight blue, a plane traverses the sky.

I watch as it's mapped by the window panes, one by one, until it disappears off the edge of the grid.

Try to will it back.

But it's gone.

And I realise I am more afraid of certainty than doubt.

Ishbel sleeps on.

I light another cigarette and wait for dawn's false promise.

# Eatin' Chicken.

*Jemma Hathaway*

Faria sighs and knocks on the door for the first time in too many years. It's the same door, only worn and flaking, and the pane is cracked. She is sure she hears the faint distantly familiar sea inside a seashell sound of a caftan against thighs, and the coconut dropped on rock of jostling beads. Beyond the crack in the glass, she sees the gathering form, sees the thundercloud swell and advance as it used to, bringing with it the suggestion of a storm. And Faria quells the old urge to hide away before it breaks. She does not want to be here.

Yolande opens the door, lacquered labyrinthine wrought iron hair, mouth a burnished chilli pepper in a pool of dark chocolate, and hooded yabettanatbelookinatmebambaclat eyes, framed by twilight shadow.

'Cha, girl.' She kisses her teeth, eyes wide. 'Seems de Lord testing me today, im bring rain wen I ang out de washin... And now im bring you.'

They stare at one another. Faria a little wriggling tadpole again, Yolande a belching, hopping frog. Yolande holds open the door, she is larger now, Faria sees, and the caftan is patched up in places.

'Ya gwan stand dere all day?'

Faria steps onto the same mat, laid on the same carpet. Yolande leads the way, great oak tree stomps, one pounding root in front of the other again and again, kadunkkadunkdunk, floorboards acquiesce to her, pictures on the wall swing keeping time, dust dances. Faria follows; she treads lightly in her Louboutins. Remembers the old fear of those feet stamping toward her. She knows they are going to the kitchen. Knows there will be plantain fermenting in the fridge, and knows she won't go near it.

'You da las person I be spectin at de door today.' Yolande draws on each word like a cigarette, her voice a pulse of saxaphonic notes, of shamanistic incantations. 'Seen ya in de paper las year. Done well for yaself girl. Dunno if I match up these days.' Yolande sneers. 'But since ya ere, ya ungry?' Her back turned, Yolande begins to cut chicken into cubes, cleaves fearlessly, blindly.

'I've eaten.'

'Makin rundown?'

'I'm a vegan.'

'You a what nuh?'

'I don't eat meat...or fish, or dairy.'

'Cha, chicken yah favourite.'

'Yeah well, that was a long time ago.'

'Mmmmm hmm.' Yolande's head moves to a private tune, eyes closed, brows raised. The chilli pepper splits, seeds spill out. 'No wonder ya like a string-bean. Lookatchoo, all bone. Huh, no man gwan eat a stick o gum for ims dinner.'

'You'd know I suppose.'

Faria sits at the kitchen table, its surface lost beneath a baize of wilting greens. Tainted pots and pans hang everywhere like tannic fruit, the linoleum flooring curls at the corners, patiently closing in on itself. She sees it all, takes it all in. Thinks of the kitchen she's used to, of the sweeping splashbacks, the Le Creuset cookware, the mirror-shine floor. Yolande tosses handfuls of spices like a conductor, douses the chicken in autumnal tinted dust.

'Whatchu doin ere?'

Faria doesn't know what to say, how to phrase the words.

'I had to come. Dad's idea, not mine.'

'Still doin everytin ya father tell ya.' Yolande's eyes make lazy cartwheels. She scrapes the chicken into a pan; it hits the heat, sizzles ragingly. This is how Faria remembers her. Back turned; hisses, steam and spit. She remembers the cooking, so much cooking. Jerk, coconut, ginger, thyme. Flavours strong enough to garnish anything. 'What im wantin me for?'

'It's still always about you, isn't it?' Faria feels the bitterness well within her again, threatening to brim over since she learnt the news that brought her here.

'Whatchu sayin to me girl?'

'You only ever cared about yourself.'

'Cha, and dat what ya come ere to tell me. Why dat take so long.'

Summer evening raindrops begin to patter at the kitchen window, like tiny bugs bursting on a windscreen at speed.

'He died.'

Yolande stops cooking. She drops the wooden spoon into the pan, cuts off the heat, sets the pan aside, covers it; a sequence of simple movements. Faria never saw her mother turn from the stove, unless food was plated.

'I ain't seen dat man in twelve years.' Yolande shuffles away, eases her big frame into the small chair alongside Faria. The wicker seat creaks beneath her. 'And sometimes I still think im gonna come through the door, sniffin out plantain, like a pig untin truffles.' Yolande shakes her head, hair immovable. Remembers when they met; remembers smoothness of skin, heat between legs.

'He was in hospital for a while…'

'And ya tell me nuthin.' Yolande inhales deeply, as if readying to breathe fire, her eyes narrow as tears creep out.

'Why would I? He left you.' Faria spits. She stands, towers like Babel over Yolande. Now Faria is the thunder, she will talk down to Yolande; dish out punishments like so many plates of sweet potato, mock the tears dry from her face. She will laugh, she will say, toughen up girl, for God sake. Ain't nobody gonna do ya no favours in this world. And then she will cook, she will cook her way through every day; she will stuff Yolande's stomach, and starve her soul. Except she can't, he made sure of that. Faria wishes she could speak to him one last time.

'Lord knows I paid for my mistakes.' Yolande relents. They look at one another, Faria with bitterness, Yolande with pain and regret. 'You said im told ya to come ere?'

Faria is back in the hospital, she sees the degrees of white and green, smells the sanitizer, hears the chatter and the moans in equal, uncomfortable measure. She sits at her father's bedside, cancer sweeps through him like sulphur. Sees him telling her what he has done. Sees him slipping away over time, unable to convince him to change his mind.

'If it was up to me I wouldn't be here, believe me. But it's out of my hands.' Faria pauses, wishing he had talked to her. 'He never stopped loving you, you know.'

'I always loved im. Only man I ever loved. Tell da truth.'

'Why do it then?' Faria shouts. 'You broke his heart.'

'I was lonely.'

'How could you be lonely, you were married.'

'Oh yes, im cared bout me, I know dat.' Yolande looks round the room, sees how little it has changed since then, except for the emptiness. 'But you, you was is true love. Seemed like de two of you was meant for each other. I neva got a look-in once you come along.' Rain pounds at the window in great, heavy pelts as though trying to get in. Yolande draws the folds of her caftan around her.

The chicken is almost cold.

Faria stares down at Yolande, realises how small she is, for so big a woman. The hair, the make-up, even the flesh, all part of a costume.

'Cha, I cook a meal every day ya know.' Yolande sighs. 'Enough to feed de dam street. Can't cook for one. A bite ere, chat sumtin sumtin dere. Dat's how it should be.' She talks almost as if to herself. 'I just keep it all in de freezer. Well, at first. Now I just throw de stuff away. No room left.'

Faria stands at the worktop, uncovers the pan. She inhales with a practiced air.

'You know he opened a Caribbean restaurant.' Faria ignites the hob, places the pan over the flame. Slowly, familiar fiery scents steal through the room.
'I seen it in de paper. Thought it was ya restaurant. Member tinkin, gosh dat sumtin special. Never thought ya give a dam bout cookin. Thought ya'd do sumtin betta. Ya wan put sum red pepper in dere now. In de cupboard just dere.'

'You never asked. Too busy shouting.' Faria winces, afraid, waits for the acid tongue to lick at her. It doesn't come. She chops the pepper, cleaves it fearlessly, blindly. 'I manage it, I don't cook.' Faria shakes her head. 'He bought it, so he could eat your food every day.'

Yolande laughs. 'Im bought a restaurant for dat. He shoulda jus come ere. Plenty in de freezer.'

'Too proud.' Faria picks a handful of the greens from the table, shreds them by hand, roughly and adds them to the pan; they shrink like magic. 'He left it to me though, the restaurant, it's all in his will.'

'Dat what ya come ere to tell me den?' Yolande's eyes darken, the black cloud threatens. 'Ya jus come to gloat or sumtin, coz I ain't got nuthin?'

'It's only mine if you agree to come and cook there. At least for a year anyway. It's binding, he was careful about that.'

'Cha.' Yolande looks out at the darkening sky, smiles. 'Ya be eatin chicken fore da year is out.'

# The Iron Plank

*Muhammad Ashfaq*

Legends of Lal Din and Allah Rakhi could not have broken out at a more opportune time for Little Commanders, who now felt tremendous heat to sustain the Order that had been created by overcoming countless hurdles, and making unmentionable sacrifices.

Commander had also started showing bitter annoyance with the way the law of the land was being violated across the Commanderate's horizons and with impunity. The regulation that people would number and not name their new-borns was being infringed. Although the majority of the citizenry still kept their tongues quiet yet abused the decree by opening their ears to whispers. Similarly, despite severe punishments, animals still mated in the open; and square-shaped houses instead of round ones had again started springing up in the far corners evidently flouting the rules. In the market, horses still fetched higher price as compared to mules despite clear-cut codes to the contrary. Some people still laughed when they were happy, and wept when they were sad; some mothers still delivered twins; rains still fell off-season; and death still ruled the roost like in the pre-insurrection era breaching the relevant regulations enforced in the Commanderate.

These were disturbing signs and Commander, in no less words, had expressed his frustration with the available armoury of powers. Little Commanders were at a loss how to further beef up Commander's power arsenal, when, to their sheer good luck, legends of Lal Din and Allah Rakhi surfaced. Fort with its awe-inspiring structure was abuzz and thrilled again. Little Commanders were regaining their lost confidence, and had started to re-group and re-assert themselves.

Today Dara Masih resembled an obnoxious, ugly, and repulsive hairy ape.

There were a couple of other equally tall, stout, and monstrous lashers waiting in the wings, but Dara Masih had been chosen for the day – and not without reason. There was a sea difference between Dara Masih and his peers, when it came to both the demonstration effect and the outcome. When Dara Masih lashed the bare backs, both the condemned and the on-lookers envisioned a spectre of the hereafter – an effect considered so very important for the decontamination of the citizenry.

Dara Masih, as was his wont, would brandish his bamboo, dance down the run-up, and scream like a bat while landing it hard at the naked surface; it was a bit of an entertainment for the spectators – anything bare and being hit, too.

This afternoon, in the midst of the lush green lawns of Fort, Dara Masih was standing tall, stiffly upright, and fully focused with his ugly hands strongly holding the bamboo lash that he had so lovingly oiled just a day ago. He was waiting for a wink to unleash himself on the deviants.

This was a settled norm in the Commanderate that all steps involved in the deliverance of justice from cognizance, investigation, litigation, adjudication, and execution were performed in one go. This was considered to be a quick and convenient system of delivery of justice to the citizenry at their doorsteps.

Commander had taken his seat in an impressive style, and nodded to initiate the proceedings. There was a pin-drop silence in the crowd, which was unusually large – given the importance of the day.

Jawans were called to bring up the first deviant.

Allah Rakhi – a shabby-looking woman – three scores and upward – barely clad and exceedingly fragile, is presented before the one-man jury – Magistrate.

"Statement of Allegations be read out loud and clear to the hear of everybody present!" Magistrate ordered commandingly.

"My Lord, this old lady, known as Allah Rakhi, the widow of that miserably dead Karam Din, in her bosom as cold as a glacier, holds the secret that is so very important for the Commanderate, its citizenry, and the Order that has been established by overcoming insurmountable hurdles." Prosecutor took a break to have an eye contact with Commander, who was peacefully perched on his throne.

Allah Rakhi in her leaning posture remained detached, calm, and motionless.

"She is known to have known and knows Saint who is known to have known and knows Flash of Acceptance that befalls during the heavenly Shab-e-Qadar…" Prosecutor continued with the Statement of Allegations.

Allah Rakhi coughed and looked for a stool, which was not there, nor made available. She leans forward a bit further.

"She is known to have met, interacted, and got blessings from Saint who guided her in how to spot Flash of Acceptance during Shab-e-Qadar…" He took a breath and gauged the audience's involvement in his argumentation.

"She is also known to have spotted Flash of Acceptance alongside Saint during Shab-e-Qadar many many years ago, and… all night… she remained with Saint!" His insinuation made with a repulsive grin, did not go well with the crowd. Prosecutor, showing no signs of embarrassment, continues.

"She out of an extreme self-centeredness, instead of imploring to Almighty for goodness and bounties for the entire citizenry, sought to serve her base self-interest!" Some of Ultra-loyalists in the crowd shouted, "Shame, Shame, Shame."

Prosecutor continues; "She is known to have demanded herself a daughter-in-law – when she still was nurturing her baby-boy in the womb – churning milk in a Silver-barrel with a Golden-rocker and a sanction to play with her grand-son!"

"What is your prayer?" Magistrate enquired visibly getting upset with Prosecutor's extended primer.

"My lord, our prayer is that Allah Rakhi be directed to divulge all information with regard to Saint so that collective benefits for the citizenry are extracted from that fellow before he vanishes into the valley of death, failing which Allah Rakhi be punished to life imprisonment with twenty-four lashes upfront." He looked at the lasher meaningfully.

Dara Masih felt itching in his hands holding the bamboo rod.

Magistrate now turned to Allah Rakhi. "What do you have to say in your defence, old lady?" Allah Rakhi apparently disoriented remained silent. Magistrate sought to frame his question differently. "What is the truth?"

She still remains silent. Commander, who is completely engrossed in the proceedings, looks towards Jawans.

A Jawan pops out of the seat and pushes Allah Rakhi in the ribs with a wooden stick. She curls. Ultra-loyalists vehemently shout; "Lash her. Lash her. Lash her."

Magistrate feeling the heat, growls at Allah Rakhi annoyingly. "What you have to say in your defence ...say something ...anything ...otherwise, I would be compelled to pronounce my judgment. So, say something before it is too late."

"Some two twenty-years ago when my man had just died by falling in the village well, he met me with his knife and dirty clothes. I gave him food and washed his clothes, and he became happy with me. He wanted to help me, if I promised not to reveal him. He thought my heart had the depth to keep the secret. During Shab-e-Qadar he prayed for me...God was kind ... and after a few months, I got the emblem of my late husband – my son – and I never shared this secret with anybody!"

"How about the Silver-barrel and the Golden-rocker, and the remaining allegations?" Magistrate enquired probingly.

"Yes, then he the most unfortunate, my only son, ran away with everything, the Silver-barrel, the Golden-rocker, and the lush woman. I don't know when he would have pity on me to bring up my grandson to play with me, and let me get rid of my now simmering and feeble body." She completed the sentence in utter dejection.

"How about Saint?" Magistrate frowned.

"I don't know. He would have died and down beneath the surface by now!" Allah Rakhi replied nonchalantly and collapsed.

Before Magistrate could pose any further questions, Ultra-loyalists clamoured again; "Lash her. Lash her. Lash her!" Prosecutor pressed the point that she had feigned fainting.

Magistrate took time, before pronouncing his judgment: "Although Allah Rakhi has been guilty of observing confidentiality of the secrets that are so very important for the smooth running of the Commanderate, its citizenry, and the Order here, yet keeping in view her old age, infirm body, and the fact that she has just fainted, it is ordained that she be put behind the bars for the rest of her life." The punishment being on the lower side did not go well with Ultra-loyalists, who raised slogans of "Shame. Shame. Shame!"

Then everything went into an eerie silence – a lull before the storm.

Suddenly, four Jawans pounce on Magistrate and punching and kicking him in the rib-cage take him away. They also drag away Allah Rakhi from the scene. In the background, Ultra-loyalists kept raising slogans: "Long Live Commander. Long Live Commander. Long Live Commander!"

When the proceedings resumed, there was New Magistrate in place, and a new deviant in the dock. Prosecutor as usual read aloud the Statement of Allegations.

"This man who is known as Lal Din is known to have known and knows Saint who is known to have known and knows to spot Flash of Acceptance during Shab-e-Qadar."

"Lal Din out of an utter greed for wealth – the very insult to the Commanderate – is known to have sought for himself an expensive iron plank, which he hid in his paddy fields and let it rust, and then, later on, was caught trying to cut it into pieces and sell – without realizing that the plank now had assumed the status of a holy relic for the entire Commanderate..." Prosecutor's eloquence had no end.

"Our prayer, my lord, thus is, that Lal Din be ordered to reveal the name of Saint, so that collective good of the Commanderate's citizenry be ensured, along with validation of confiscation of the iron plank." Looking at New Magistrate, Prosecutor concluded his inquisition.

New Magistrate turned to Lal Din with a visibly belligerent tone: "What is the truth, Cheat?"

Lal Din, as if, was looking for an opportunity. "Well, one day I was planking my paddy fields in the afternoon, when he with a knife in his hands passed by; he was going to another far village, I thought. He was thirsty and hungry. My wife had just brought me food. I shared my bread and milk with him, and he was happy. He told me he was Saint. I said 'it is ok'. He asked me if I wanted anything. I asked him to pray for my ailing buffalo. He laughed. He was more happy with me and asked for something more. I didn't know what to ask, and then he said the falling night was Shab-e-Qadar and I could get anything I wanted. I still didn't know what to ask. He advised me that I could even get that plank of mine turned gold. I thought he joked. I refused because then how would I plank my fields. My wife laughed. He told me I was a dude, and I might not then need planking at all. My wife was happy. He advised me to lift the plank on my shoulder and keep saying; 'Oh, You owner of Shab-e-Qadar turn it gold...; Oh, You owner of Shab-e-Qadar turn it gold...; Oh, You owner of Shab-e-Qadar turn it gold!' Saint said I had to keep it repeating quickly because Flash of Acceptance was only very very small. Saint started offering his prayers. He kept offering prayers all night. It was quite tough and my wife gave me water. I remember I stood all night and one of my sheep gave two baby lambs that night. Late mid-night my shoulder tired, but his prayers did not come to an end. Whole night standing with a plank on your shoulder is not easy, but my wife encouraged me and I stood. She managed the cattle. How long...? My shoulder swelled. It was painful. I felt my shoulder would break. Saint was there to identify me Flash of Acceptance, but he did not...he kept praying. Tired, I threw my plank down saying hell with gold...turn iron...and it turned iron...It was my bad luck...I am not sure about trees, and animals, but Saint was prostrating."

New Magistrate growled. "I am not interested in tales man; where is Saint?"

"How would I know?" Lal Din retorted.

"Did he advise you to keep his identity confidential?" New Magistrate questioned.

"Yes, he said to me but that was many years ago, and how would I remember him even if I want to? I don't think I know him anymore? So may I go now as I have to feed my buffalos; they would be hungry?" Lal Din's hurry further fuelled New Magistrate's ire. His wink was good for a judgment to bring Dara Masih into the act.

Lal Din did not budge an inch for the full quota of a dozen whips. This was unusual. This had never happened to Dara Masih; the target would start uttering the wanted words much before the pronounced punishment had been awarded fully. He looked at New Magistrate enquiringly, who obliged him with a nod of his head that meant extension in punishment by one hundred per cent. According to the decree of Commander, Magistrate carried a carte blanche – he could change, increase, decrease the quantum and nature of punishment to any level for any deviant, but was responsible to produce positive results. The hunter could become hunted in no time in the Commanderate, so he had to be careful. His predecessor-in-office had just been sent to jail on charges of conniving and commiserating with a deviant.

"Where is Saint?" New Magistrate fumed after the twentieth whip. He was afraid of losing Lal Din along with that critical information Commander needed so desperately to restore Order.

"I don't know!" Lal Din murmured after that fierce hit.

"You shut up bastard ... it can't be." Magistrate got out of his elevated dais and kicked him between the legs irritably.

"Ok! Let it be so..." Lal Din said resignedly.

"Who and where is Saint?" New Magistrate growled and slapped Lal Din in the face.

"Which Saint you are talking about – he was just a passer-by. I don't know him anymore. I swear I don't know him. Now let me go; my wife alone cannot feed the cattle!" Visibly broken Lal Din pleaded.

Dara Masih sensing success, hopped for the next strike.

This stalemate came to an end when Lal Din's bare back bled badly, and he felt they would take him like in cases of so many people he knew and then they were never heard of. This terrified him. Lal Din thought he was a man of his words; but he had been caught and lashed brutally. He commiserated with Saint.


Decree for Saint's arrest was immediately issued, but Commander's camp increasingly felt frustrated as Shab-e-Qadar was now fast approaching.

After a few days, Saint was nabbed with his knife from a remote shrine. He was brought all fours tied and presented before Commander for an in-camera Summary Trial.

Summary Trial Court was headed by Commander himself under the law he had kept unto himself.

The Statement of Allegations was read out but Saint had no defence.

According to the judgment delivered, Saint would stay confined in Contemplation Cell, and help Commander spot Flash of Acceptance during Shab-e-

Qadar, and if he successfully discharged this obligation, his freedom might be considered. However, if he failed in his purpose, he would be condemned to the darkest cell for life.

"Do you accept the judgment?" Enquired Commander.

"Knowing that there is no alternative, I do!" Said Saint curtly.

"What would then be your strategy toward achieving the objectives?" Commander was straight.

"Depends upon what are your objectives?" Saint confronted him firmly.

"Power – more power only – and that too for the betterment, and goodness of my citizenry, and not, of course, for myself." Commander replied altruistically.

"Power! I mean what do you want?" Saint asked confusedly.

Commander had to concentrate hard: "Whatever I Command Is Executed!"

Saint visibly shivers.

"O, Saint! You would stay with me in Contemplation Cell till Shab-e-Qadar is over. You would pray for me, and spot me Flash of Acceptance. You would neither yawn nor sleep, nor miss out on Flash of Acceptance and squander the golden opportunity to empower your Commander for the collective good of the citizenry!"

Saint interrupted him. "This is not right. If you want acceptance of your prayers, you should pray all night and in return, God would – may oblige."

This hugely annoyed Commander. "Look Saint I told you I have only one desire, one ultimate desire: Whatever I Command Is Executed. Look it is very simple; I don't think God should have any problems with such a tiny little desire of mine. I am not asking for a planet. I don't want anything for myself, but I want more power for doing well to my subjects. I want them to give everything they want. This is a sublime objective of my life, and Saint you would – whether you like it or not – are going to make it happen. You keep the key, Saint!"

A Little Commander rose up and grabbed Saint from his long untidy and uncombed hair. "Don't you ever think of running away. We would dig you out from under the soil and pull you down from the skies. We may have grown weaker but are still more powerful than you – than anybody around. Don't at all underestimate our outreach, Saint!"

"Look, it eventually has to be yourself – awake, attentive, and begging when Flash of Acceptance happens during Shab-e-Qadar. All trees, animals and living things would instinctively prostrate. That is when you articulate your desire and God may oblige you!" Saint explained.

Commander was not impressed with the prescription. "Oh. If I were to keep awake all night and pray, why the hell do I have you, Saint?" Commander retorted belligerently.

He looks around and a couple of Jawans close in and encircle Saint intimidatingly. This softens up Saint, and a common ground is found. Commander, under Saint's active supervision, rehearsed to articulate his desire loud and fast: "Whatever I Command Is Executed. Whatever I Command Is Executed. Whatever I Command Is Executed." Saint remained shut inside Contemplation Cell with an absolute guard around.

Soon, Shab-e-Qadar arrived; it was a breath-taking wait. The citizenry did not sleep. Little Commanders held their breaths. The Commanderate was motionless in entirety, none moved out of his house, none ploughed, none planked, none talked, none looked at Fort from his roof-top. Everyone was awed to death that night. It was not a night like any other night.

In the morning, when Little Commanders anxiously barge into Contemplation Cell, they find Commander's body lying cold in a pool of blood. Saint is gone; Contemplation Cell's mighty walls exhibit a hole of Saint's size with his knife dug deep inside Commander's blood-soaked bosom.
A blood-scribbled note pasted on Commander's fore-head reads: "Gods Don't Replicate, Dude!"
Fort's gates were crashed, walls razed to the ground in no time, and people took away whatever fell their way.
At noon time, Lal Din also came and took away his iron plank.

## Dancefloor in Outer Space

*Paul G. Duke*

*Wake up you idiot.*
My eyes flutter open, sticky with the rust of a deep sleep. I have no idea how long I've been out, but my toes are frozen numb and pressing out against the hard leather of my work boots.
*You're lucky that Mrs.Greenhat was harmless.*
The old lady in the green hat, who had been sitting next to me in the window seat since we left Thunder Bay, is gone. In her place now is a Chinese woman.
*You weren't supposed to fall asleep. Now there's a Chinese beside you.*
Sweat forms in my ears and above my lip. I squeeze my hands into bricks and my head freezes, aimed straight ahead, like the marble statue of some wartime general.
*Change seats before it's too late!*

It was all over the TV that week. News reports of the murder of a young man named Tim McLean, killed while on a bus crossing the Prairies through the heart of the country. Murdered by the passenger sitting next to him, the mentally disturbed Vincent Weiguang Li. At some point, Li had snapped turned a concealed "Rambo" knife on Tim McLean, decapitating him. He even displayed the kid's head to the other passengers.

That same week, I had dropped out of school. My school was a total dump. Mind you, working at the Thunder Bay Steelworks wouldn't be much better, but getting a job there was my only real option, and I figured that at least, I'd be able to afford to buy as much music as I wanted. I planned to get my own place, a nice stereo system, and play whatever music I liked as loud as I wanted, and to hell with the kids from school. Those losers only ever listened to rock music, and they teased me for digging Jazz. Fuck 'em.

"It's all part of God's master plan for you son," said my father, not the least unpleased at the news of my dropping out. In fact, he was so eager to get me hired on at the Steelworks, where he himself had been working for thirty years, that he put the word in for me with his boss the next day. But the Steelworks weren't hiring. They were about to lay off three hundred workers, my father being one of them.

So we called up my Uncle Rollie, who lives out west in Vancouver. He said sure, send the boy out and he'd get me hired on at the pulp mill where he was a foreman. God's master plan may have turned to shit in Thunder Bay, but out west were beaches, surfing and hippies and nobody there knew me. In a place like that, I could be who I wanted to be.

The night before I was to leave Thunder Bay though, the news of the Prairie Murder hit the media, and my parents freaked out.

"This Li is Chinese," said my mother, horrified. "Maybe they just don't take to our land. Maybe the open space does something to them?"

"How in God's name does a monster like that get into our country?" said my father. "He should have been locked up in a cage."

My mother suggested I should stay; try to get back into school.

"It's not as if the kid's especially bright, and he doesn't seem to have any special talents for much," said my father. He was probably right. "The kid needs to find a job before the Chinas take 'em all away. You turn your back on the godless bastards for a second, they go and take the bloody factories to bloody China. God-damned shame it is."

"Godless bastards," my mother concurred.

"Don't worry son," my father said. "We'll get you to Vancouver."

Later that night, my father handed me something wrapped in a green cloth bundle. "God makes the evil ones, but he also makes the good ones too," he said. "It's time to be your own man son."

Between the folds of soft cloth was his favorite hunting knife, a six-inch military-issue Bowie, snug in its brown leather scabbard. I slid the blade out.

"Your uncle says he'll meet you at the A&W inside the Vancouver bus terminal. If you get there early, just sit tight and wait for him. Got it?"

I nodded, staring at the gleaming steel in my hand, hypnotized by the power suggested by the gentle curve of its razor-edge.

"Listen to me son," his eyes found mine. "You keep your eyes open out there. The world is full of perverts and murderers. Watch for strangers. Foreigners, you know what I mean? Anybody makes a move on you, don't hesitate. Strike first."

I nodded.

*No evil Chinese madman is going to mess with you now. Strike first.*

The next morning, I boarded the bus, and found at the very back the only vacant seat left. In the window-seat next to me was this old lady with a huge green hat, one of those crazy Queen of England numbers. At first, she tried with the hello-son-where-are- you-heading stuff, but when I stuck the earphones of my iPod in and cranked some John Coltrane, she left me alone.

I'm seventeen, and it's the first time I've travelled anywhere on my own.

The only Chinese women I've ever seen are in Kung-Fu movies, where they hide swords in their hair, and slice men in half while they drink at roadside teahouses. But this one doesn't look much like a Kung-fu killer. She's sound asleep, with her head resting against the window. She has on an expensive-looking dark overcoat, and her lower legs are sealed in glossy black boots. She makes no sound, and is so completely still she could be an ice sculpture. For the moment, she looks harmless enough, but like my father always says, that's the thing about the Chinese; they're sneaky and deceitful.

*Your father is right. Don't trust her appearance.*

Grabbing my backpack, I stagger to the front of the bus. The bus driver is a huge round man. Long white hairs curl out of his ears like whiskers on a big drunken cat, and he reeks of coffee. The steering wheel looks ready to collapse in the vice-grip of the driver's thick powerful fingers. I ask him how long until we reach the next stop, and he tells me maybe four hours 'til Winnipeg.

"Better get comfortable kid," he says.

"But there's a-"

The driver flashes a red eye toward me, then sets it back to the road ahead. "There's a what?"

I feel suddenly childish. Like I'm running for help. No wonder my parents think I'm useless. "Never mind," I say.

The prospect of sitting beside the Chinese woman for the whole trip, four days from Thunder Bay to Vancouver, fills me with an icy dread. As I pass the other passengers, I notice that most of them are old folks, some asleep, some chatting quietly amongst themselves. They don't seem the least concerned that there's a Chinese woman on the bus. I'm clearly the youngest one on the bus; so it's up to me. I'll have to keep my eyes on her the whole time, maintain an unwavering vigil. I'm the sentry.

While I'm still up, I stretch my arms and roll shoulders. My movements have no effect on the Chinese woman. She remains still as steel against the window.

*Its part of God's master plan for you son. You've been granted a sacred duty.*

*Remember, the Chinese can't be trusted for a second. She makes one move toward you, you stab her eyes out.*

I take my seat and adjust my posture until I'm reasonably comfortable. I set my backpack on the floor in front of me. On my birthday, my mother gave me a pair of new Kodiak work-boots. They're not worked-in yet, and have begun to really sting my feet. I want to stretch them out to rest on the backpack, but that would jeopardize my chances of reacting quickly to any attack, so I plant them on the floor below me instead. I cushion my head to one side, so the Chinese woman is clear in my sight. In the window beyond her, the rusting factories and brick smokestacks I've lived amongst my whole life blur past, reduced now to formless streaks of orange and brown.

By nightfall, we're into the Prairies. Everyone on the bus is asleep, hidden from me by the shadows and seats. From behind, even the driver looks asleep-his hands are welded to the steering wheel at perfect "Tens and Twos." I seem to be the only one awake. I think about Vancouver. How different life will be. No more school, no more parents nagging me. I'll get my own apartment; date the girls I want to, surf, snowboard, climb mountains. Maybe I can find a night job in a jazz bar, something cool like that.

The front of the bus strikes it first. Then the back lurches up and I bounce out of my seat. My iPod slams to the floor. We've hit something. Everyone's awake now; the whole bus is buzzing with confusion. The bus squeals to a stop and the driver steps off.
A few moments pass silently before the driver returns, swinging the door shut behind him with a metallic creak. "Sorry folks," he announces with a

deep loud voice. "Mafia dumps a lot of bodies out here. Nothing to worry about."

The bus goes even more silent, if that's possible. In the rear-view mirror, I see the driver, who winks at me and grins. "Just kidding. Dead Coyote."

I laugh for a moment, but then I notice that, incredibly, aside from a few strands of hair that have strayed across her face, neither the bouncing bus nor the noise of the passengers have any effect on the Chinese woman. If anything, she somehow looks even more asleep.

*Don't be fooled. It's some ancient Kung-Fu meditation thing. She knows you're watching her.*

For the first time, the thought strikes me; maybe the Chinese woman's not asleep at all. Maybe she's dead. My hand reaches into my jacket and my fingers wrap around the handle of my knife. I'm terrified, but ready. Careful not to disturb the air molecules between us, I lean over and turn an ear to the lapel of her overcoat.

An amazing scent greets my nose as I enter the range of her perfume, and the tension washes out of me. I ease my ear closer still. Her chest heaves with the slightest whispers. She's breathing, but is this normal breathing? How would I know? Maybe Chinese breathe differently.

*Are you crazy? Pull your head away from her!*

Maybe she's drugged, spaced-out on pills or something. Images from Kung-Fu movies form in my mind: old Chinatowns, where sad fallen concubines smoke away their shame in gloomy dank opium dens. With my head at her chest, she could easily grab me in a choke-hold if she woke. This thought focuses in me, even as I notice the soft pale skin showing above the V-line of the white blouse she's wearing under the coat. I pull my eyes downward, across the slender darkness of her coat, and see that she's also wearing around her thin wrist an expensive-looking watch. A Gucci. Hardly a sign of someone "fallen." All said and done, she doesn't really look dangerous, and she sure doesn't smell it. She looks more like a collection agent from the bank, or the owner of a fancy shop. Maybe she's crossing the country, buying homes. My mother says pretty soon regular Canadians won't be able to afford a home, because all the rich Chinese are buying them and raising the prices. I pull my head away from her chest.

*So she's got fancy clothes. She might be a secret agent. A spy. An assassin. Look at the way she wears her coat, buttoned all the way to the top. She's concealing a weapon for sure.*

Across the aisle from me, a middle-aged businessman in a suit and tie, who's been snoring for the past few hours, wakes up. He smiles and squeezes past me on his way to the washroom at the rear of the bus.

Questions simmer up to the forefront of my mind. When had this woman boarded the bus? How had she managed to take the seat beside me, the window seat that, without my being aware of it? Had she climbed over top of me? How could I not have noticed *that*?

*They're sneaky. I told you, they have ways.*

She's like one of those giant crane towers on construction sites, the ones that run up through the centre of a building while it's being built. You never see them arrive. Never see them erected or assembled or even being lowered into place by a helicopter. One day, they're simply there, and you are forced to live with the mystery.

*No mystery about it. She took Mrs. Greenhat's seat right from under her. She took what didn't belong to her.*

The businessman returns to his seat. He smiles again and turns his gaze to the Chinese woman. His eyes trace a line from the woman's boots all the way up to her hair. "Where you heading son?"

For a moment, I pretend I can't hear him over the music, but he holds his gaze on me. I pop one of the earpieces out. "Vancouver."

"Long trip," he gestures to the Chinese woman with a nod. "Wanna switch seats?"

There's something lewd and ugly about the way he looks at her; he reminds me of a hunter, starving from weeks in the wilderness, coming across an extra-large pizza. He smells of stale tobacco and booze. He's creepy.

"No thanks," I say.

A few hours later, my eyes burning and dry, we arrive at Winnipeg Station. Smothering everything is a thick blanket of snow. The passengers leave the bus and head into the small grey terminal building, where a Tim Horton's donut shop and public washrooms wait for them. The Chinese woman still doesn't awaken.

I wait for the stinky businessman to leave, then I too step off the bus and into the bracing chill outside. I buy myself a large coffee at the Horton's.

After a half hour, the bus engine rumbles back to life. I take my seat beside the Chinese woman. The hot aroma of my coffee kills off the floral breeze of the woman. The businessman takes his seat too.

That's Winnipeg, I think. Not much to it. As the bus twists out of the station, I watch through the window as fresh snow blows up in soft gusts, and swirling against the glass they form the pale faces of prairie history's ghosts, each of them staring back at me.

God is putting me to the test.

*That's right. You've got to protect the others. God's given you this duty. Time to be your own man.*

I don't know how many hours later, the prairie morning appears outside. It's an endless white horizon scrolling by. Mile after mile of nothingness.

We stop briefly in Saskatoon, and everybody gets out to stretch and breathe the fresh air. The tiny bus terminal is virtually empty. I notice only a single person working there, a lone ticket agent, an old man who sips coffee and stares into a TV. What a dump, I think, how does anybody live there, and I'm relieved when we pull out and move on toward Calgary.

The day dissolves into night before my eyes, now burning and dry with fatigue. When they start to drop, I try propping them open with my fingers, and inhale long, deep breaths until I feel energized once again. This works for a while, but gradually this technique fails me. Sleep seems to reach out and claw at me, determined to drag me into its dark world. But I can't let that happen. The Chinese woman might wake up, and slaughter me in my sleep or take my job.

Outside the bus, even though the sun glows strong and bright- its morning already?- the endless white nothingness of the prairie day threatens to lull me into the same dark world that the Chinese woman seems unable to leave. I fight its hypnotic force with every atom of will I have.

*No matter what, you must stay awake. Your life and the lives of the others depend on it. If you can't take it anymore, you'll have to eliminate the threat before you sleep.*

Repeatedly, I stretch open my fingers and quickly squeeze them shut, and gradually breathe some life back into my frozen limbs.

The Chinese woman's pale skin is still pressed against the cold glass when night comes again. A thick darkness envelops everything outside the bus like some super-massive Black Hole swallowing the sun. The cast from the interior lights of the bus turn the window pressed against the woman's face into a cold dark mirror, and in it I see my own wasting face inches from hers, our noses almost touching. The "I" that I am in the reflection doesn't look afraid. In reverse, my face looks...pleased.

I can't tell her age, maybe thirty. Girls that I know show their age in the thickness of the potato chip-and-pizza fat at their necks, but this woman wears a timeless slender. She could be as young as twenty, or much older than that. The girls back home were flasks of cheap vodka at the football game, but this woman is clearly an evening of theatre followed by champagne cocktails at jazzy piano lounges. She looks the way Stan Getz, Gerry Mulligan, pre-heroin Chet Baker, and Miles Davis sound. Elegant. Cool.

*Stop that! It's one of her tricks, so don't fall for it. Keep your mind right.*

Feeling myself lulled into ease by her handsome appearance, I snap myself out of it with a stretch of my jaw muscles, and a few deep breaths. The snow streaks past the window in horizontal fingers that snatch time itself into its grasp, only to be smashed and melted against the heated metal hull of the speeding bus. All that remains in its absence is a deep cold that at least has the effect of sharpening my focus on the Chinese woman even more.

My feet are killing me. They're swollen and trying to burst. I untie my boots, slip my aching feet out, and with a deep sigh of relief, set them to rest upon the backpack. I wiggle my toes, hoping to move some blood out of my feet and back into my mind. A fatigue has taken residence inside me, dense and alive as if another person, a demon of some kind, has burrowed under my skin and displaced me altogether.

Somewhere in the middle of the prairies, she moves.

Her hips turn away from the window, her arms fold across her chest, one hand clutching a blue leather handbag. Her head shifts until it's pointed in my direction. Her eyes are still closed, but she seems to be staring at me through her eyelids. The far quarter of her face remains veiled by a few strands of black hair, but her new angle permits the clearest view of her yet, and though she's as asleep as ever, something about her takes on new life.

I think of my hometown, so far away now and struggling to survive its loss of industry. And my parents. If I had stayed, the burden on them would have been too much. They're now free of me, but somehow, even a thousand miles from them, I don't really feel free of them. From their absurd faith in God, Industry, and this place called Canada, which from where I am sitting, is nothing more than a vast sheet of plain white paper. The Prairies are a real dump. And somewhere out here on this same highway, amidst the same expanse of lifeless cold, another young guy riding a bus had crossed paths with a monster. How could any God create such a violent evil and just stick it out there on the prairies like that, waiting to trap innocent lives?

It's like some sick cosmic joke.

Calgary comes and goes. I don't even get off the bus. My legs wouldn't hold me up anyway-they've gone completely numb. Now I too, feel frozen in my seat.
Vancouver is only ten hours away now...gotta stay awake.
*That's right, no matter what, stay awake.*
Stay awake.

The bus makes it out of the Prairies and we head upward into the Rocky Mountains. The air flowing into my lungs thins and my breath grows shallow. The hunger that had until now merely annoyed me is now burning a hole in my belly. While wondering how the Chinese woman can sleep so long without eating, the thought occurs to me that maybe she has some food in her handbag.
No longer able to control myself, I reach over to her handbag and gently pry open its tiny metal clasp. Inside are a cell phone, a make-up kit, and a small plastic package of Cherry Nibs. It's my hunger that does it, moves into the purse and lifts the Nibs out.
She doesn't notice. I hold the Nibs in my hand, they look fresh and delicious; certain to ease the pain in my gut. But what if she wakes and finds her snack

removed from her purse? She'll tell the driver who will beat them out of me. I'll be arrested for my hunger and desperation.

*So what if you take her Nibs? What's she gonna do about it? Remember, you're the one with a knife.*

But I can't bring myself to eat them. I just sit there holding the plastic package in my lap. Tired of supporting the growing weight of the knife in my chest pocket, I pull it out and stuff it into my backpack. I can still reach it if I need to, I figure. This way, I can curl my hand into the warmth of my jacket without touching the thing.

We're surrounded by tall green trees. Maybe, I can't tell; it's all just a haze that swirls into my mind until eventually the last of my focus drifts. My eyelids, heavier than I can hold up any longer, finally close, as sleep overtakes me and I'm swallowed up by a darkness that's as thick as prehistoric tar. I'm tumbling through outer space. Silent. Cold. But this outer space has no stars and no planets. No moons or meteors. There's no sound and no texture, nothing I can touch or feel, just a deep, black, nothingness.

But being weightless feels great. I try to relax, and whistle a half-decent rendition of Gerry Mulligan's *Body and Soul*, into the darkness around me, where the notes shatter into the vacuum. Then, something tugs on my legs, a force of some kind, pulling me in some direction, maybe down? I'm moving faster and faster toward something. My face ripples; my skin stretches like a rubber balloon. I see in the distance a tiny speck of light. I'm falling towards it, accelerating with impossible speed, until I'm close enough to see clearly what it really is. It's a wide, flat surface, lit with a thousand coloured lights.

And riding it, as though it's an enormous circular surfboard, is the sleeping Chinese woman. Only she's awake, and she's not surfing. She's dancing. On a gigantic disco dancefloor.

What the hell?

I brace myself for the coming impact. The woman is still dancing, and doesn't see me coming. I'm heading right for her. With incredible force, I slam into the dancefloor, right at her feet.

She jumps back.

"Hey, you're awake," is all I can come up with. She pulls away without saying a word. Maybe she can't speak English. Or maybe she doesn't recognize me. I glance down and check myself for any anthropological irregularities, but I look the same as always: jacket, jeans, Kodiak work boots. "It's only me. I sat beside you on the bus?"

"I can't talk to you," she says, and walks away from me, heading off across the lighted floor.

I try a compliment. I'm not sure why, but I feel the need to speak with her. "You speak pretty good English for a Chinese girl."

She stops. "I'm not Chinese, idiot. I'm Canadian."

"Oh," I mumble, feeling stupid. "It's just that, I've been wanting to talk to you."

The woman takes several steps back. "I can't do that."

"Because I'm...not Chinese?"

She shakes her head. "You're a stranger in here. A foreigner. So I have to be careful."

"I'm not the least bit harmless. I just wanted to meet you."

"Why?" She bites her lower lip, puzzling something over. She brushes her black hair away from her eyes. "I don't know what it is, but there's something about you that's just, *wrong.*"

"Wrong?"

She nods her head. "Wait. What sort of music do you listen to?"

"Well, I like Jazz."

"Jazz?" her eyes widen, and a hesitant smile breaks at the corner of her lips. "I like jazz too. That can't be it then."

I smile. She likes Jazz.

*She doesn't look like a jazz fan. She-*

"Who said that?" she stiffens.

"Hey, I've been wanting to ask you. Why do you sleep so much on the bus?"

"Maybe I'm afraid of you."

*Why the hell should she be afraid of you? She's Chinese, she's the foreigner.*

Her head spins. "There it is again." Before I realize what is happening, the woman has reached into my jacket, and pulls out the knife.

"How dare you bring that thing in here?"

I struggle to find an answer.

She throws the knife to the floor as if it were white-hot. Her eyes widen with terror.

*Quick, stab her eyes out! Assault the ambush. Pre-emptive strike.*

The knife begins to shake, vibrating as though it's about to explode. Then - and I can't believe what I'm seeing - a thin line splits the knife down its length, and it *hatches.*

"Look what you've done," She runs at me and with her fist and pounds at my chest, but gives up and I put an arm around her and she accepts the gesture, burying her face in the curve of my inner shoulder. I can smell her magic perfume again, a scent like nothing else.

What comes oozing out of the knife is formless at first. A slimy blob. With amazing speed, it seems to catch its breath and grow, taking the shape first of a featureless infant, a small boy, then finally, it raises an adult head and looks directly at us. It is not quite a complete human, just a smooth *form,* and I recognize it from TV. It's Vincent Weiguang Li. Or rather, his form. A Li-form. It stoops down and picks up the two pieces of the knife, and squeezes them back into its original deadly shape.

The woman grabs my hand and pulls me to the centre of the dancefloor.

"How'd he get in here?" I say, sweat pooling at my back.

She turns and glares. "You brought him in."

"I did?"

A giant iPod appears, and immediately starts playing Baden Powell's "Blues A Volente." The Li-form advances toward us, brandishing the knife above its shoulder.

She swings me around.

"Dance."

As we dance, the entire dancefloor begins to rotate around us. I feel dizzy. The Li-form is only a few steps from us now. Her feet slide gracefully over the coloured lights. I follow, doing my best not to trip on my boots. The Li-form stabs at the woman, but misses as she turns into a pirouette. We're spinning faster now, and the centrifugal force pushes against him. He stumbles and falls to his feet, but again slides further away, struggling to hold onto the floor. I get a clear look at the creature. His face is void of any human features, his skin looks made of translucent grey jello, and his eyes are solid black holes. But looking into his expressionless face, my perception shifts, and I see *my own face.*

"I" come into focus: my wavy brown hair, my green eyes and big ears. The Li-form, or Me-form, whatever it is, is even wearing my Kodiak boots.

"Faster," cries the woman. "Don't stop yet."

I don't know what I'm doing, but I let the music, and the beautiful woman, take me into their flow. I dance faster, wilder, swinging my limbs with more...grooviness?

"Gosh," she says, a gleam of surprise in her eyes. "You're a good dancer."

"I've never danced before," I confess. "The whole endeavour is absurd to me."

"I'll show you absurd," she says, and with a swing of her long black hair, she spins me into a pirouette.

The dancefloor lurches and accelerates into another gear. The Li-Me-Whatever-form makes a final, desperate slash of the knife across empty space, and then careens off the dancefloor, and is sucked out into space. In seconds, he's a tiny speck vanishing into the dark void.

We're alone again, safe. We stop dancing and catch our breaths. I bite for air. She seems fine, her breathing calm. She's clearly in far better condition than I am.

She touches a hand to my shoulder. "I'm hungry," she says. A low dining table appears, covered with dishes of food. She takes my hand and pulls me down to the table. "Do you like sushi?"

"I've never had sushi before, but I'll try it." I feel the urge to tell her how I stole the Cherry Nibs from her purse, but I'm afraid of losing her so, I hesitate. "If you're Chinese, how come you eat Japanese food?"

"How do you know I'm Chinese?" she smiles. "Maybe I am Japanese."

"Are you?"

"You really are an idiot."

"Yup."

She folds her legs under the table and sits. I follow suit; my legs ache with stiffness from the long travel. She slides a plate in front of me. A pulpy orange blob sits on top of an open shell with three-inch black spikes sticking out all around it. I stuff the thing whole it into my mouth. The woman bursts into a laugh. "You're not supposed to eat the shell, silly."

But it tastes wonderful, like the ocean, and makes my body feel warm and pleasant. The spikes poke out through my neck.

"It's sea urchin. *Uni.*"

"Uni?" I say, the movement in my neck causing the spikes to wiggle. "Tasty."

After dinner, we're at the edge of the dancefloor peering out through the curtain of space. For some reason, I feel a deep, heavy sense of loss. Loss of what I can't tell, it's just a feeling that sits like a limestone rock in the pit of my stomach. What have I lost? I'm just beginning my life. "You said I'm a stranger, a foreigner, in here. But *where* is here?"

"The farthest edge of the universe," she explains. "Yet, also it's very centre. The place where everything converges. The great Nothing."

"Kinda like a black hole?"

She nods. "The Nothing side."

"The Nothing side of what?"

"Everything."

I let this swim around in my head for a moment, until the sloshing makes me seasick. "I think now I really have absolutely no idea what you mean."

"Energy, life even, can only contract so much. Once things get sucked in, they squeeze through a sort of tunnel, and, reaching their maximum contraction state, burst through this wormhole deal and out the other side in a huge expansion of energy."

I never did well in physics class, but it sort of seems familiar to me. The woman is smart. I want to ask her what she knows about construction cranes.

"It's not physics, but yet it is." She continues. "Time, space, up, down, light and dark, yin, yang, in, out; Eros and Thanatos, if you prefer Freudian terms. Sex, violence; love, hate; creation, destruction. Each one its own complement, expanding and contracting. Alternating contradictions. Paradoxes folding into themselves."

"How about good and evil? How do they work in here?"

"Everything is in here, in ever-flowing oscillation."

"What about when people die, do they come out here? I mean, *in* here?" I don't know what I mean. But I want to know.

"They return to Nothing," she lowers her eyes and gently nods. And for the first time, I notice her, really notice *her*. It's as if I'm seeing her for the first time. She's about twenty-six. Her black hair falls to the shoulders of her black overcoat and spreads across them like the leaves of a weeping willow in the moonlight. The soft, grey fur of her overcoat's hood frame her alabaster face like a fox curled around a stolen pearl. A gold necklace, thin as a leaf held sideways, hangs over the pale skin visible at her neckline. Her narrow eyes are open just so, a thin veil of blue shadow above them. Her delicate black eyelashes stroke the air in front of her. Her eyes are so thin I can't help wondering if she can see as much of the world as I can. The gentle pout of her lips are a soft, remote red. The tips of her ears piercing the veil of black hair are two pale flowers in the early moments of their spring blossom. Her nose rises from her face so subtly, is such a gentle hill of snow that it's impossible to say where it begins or ends.

A guilty hand slaps me out of the lyrical mood. "I better go now."

"Why do you go?" She takes my hand in hers and looks into my eyes. I was right. She's beautiful when she's awake, too.

"I have to get to Vancouver. Someone's waiting for me."

"Stay," she says, smiling at me.

But I slide my hand from hers, turn, and leap off the dancefloor.

I wake to a sharp pain in my foot. When I look down at it, I see that my foot is impaled on the knife. Somehow the knife has escaped the scabbard and while my foot lay on the backpack, the blade sunk into my sole, stabbing a small gash under my big toe. A bloody smear has soaked into my sock. A pain of a different sort stabs me too.

She's gone. The seat beside me is empty for the first time on my trip. It looks like a massive crater, or an ocean drained of its waves. Emptiness. I still have her Cherry Nibs too and won't be able to give them back to her. When she left, she must have noticed me holding them. She must have seen them. And yet she didn't take them from me.

*They're probably laced with poison, arsenic or something, that's why.*
*Whatever you do, don't eat them.*

I lift the knife and wipe it off on my sock, already bloodied. As I jam the knife back into its scabbard, the squeeze of the fit tells me there's no way it could have simply slid out.

*She did it. She pulled me out of your pocket and turned me against you. She made me, the Chinese woman.*

How do I even know she's Chinese? And if she had reached into my backpack, I would have noticed.

*You were tired, you stayed awake too long. You were dead tired. Knocked out. She moved like a cat, and you didn't notice. She did it. You missed her attack.*

Shut up.

I shoulder my backpack and leave the bus. Outside, I meet the driver. He's alone, kneeling under the back of the bus, attending to some small repair.

"Did you happen to see which way that Asian woman went?" I ask.

"Asian woman?" he pulls himself up from the pavement. "What'd she look like?"

"I don't know, she was sorta pretty," I say. "For a Chinese girl, I mean."

"Don't recall kid."

"She was asleep the whole time." My Nikes squeak on the wet concrete. "Did you see which way she went after she got off the bus?"

The Driver shrugs and shakes his head. "I wouldn't sweat it kid. This town is full of Asian girls.

Dime a dozen. Chinese, Korean, Japanese. All the major brands available here," he laughs at this.

"But I need to return these to her," I hold out the Cherry Nibs.

The driver chuckles and shakes his head and I realize how much he resembles a grotesque alien beetle.

Inside the station are hundreds of people, greetings and goodbyes everywhere. Scanning the crowd, I search for her black hair and those thin gentle eyes that I've never seen open. But the driver is right. At least half of the people are Asians, and I can't find her anywhere among them. Seeing so many Asian people amassed in one place like that is overwhelming, and I realize that they could be Chinese, Korean, Japanese or Vietnamese, and I wouldn't even know the difference. In that place, smiling and hugging each other, they all seem like one family. Two of their number hurry by me, holding hands and smiling briefly in my direction, despite the fact that here I am the foreigner.

I locate the A&W, but Uncle Rollie is nowhere to be seen. I buy some lunch and find a seat among the crowd. The two Teen Burgers and chocolate shake I buy do nothing to ease the bottomless hunger that has opened inside me.

*Consider yourself lucky she didn't murder you when you fell asleep. Now that you're in Vancouver, you mustn't let your guard down ever again.*

You're lying. Why are you lying? Why have you lied to me? She's harmless. She did nothing to me. She's...

*Yes, what?*

She's harmless and...

*Don't let your father and mother down. Don't disgrace them. The Chinese stole your father's job, and they'll steal yours too. You can't trust them. They're taking all the factories to China, they're cheating at the Olympics, they kill whales and make coca cola out of girl's hair. They eat their babies, they tie women's feet up, export heroin all over the world, finance communist guerrilla armies. Half the guns in the world are built in China. Stay with your own kind! This town is full of them, you gotta protect yourself. Your father wanted me to protect you from them.*
...she's beautiful.

I toss the burger wrappers in the garbage and leave the A&W. The Guard on duty at the Security desk is a large man with short hair and a professional scowl, which he turns on me. "May I help you sir?"

I slide the green cloth bundle across his desk, anxious to be free of its weight.

"What this?" he asks, taking the knife in his hand.

"Somebody left it on the bus."

Outside the station, it's pouring with rain. Downtown Vancouver waits for me a few blocks away, a dense forest of apartment towers and office buildings, gleaming with the wet winter day. Poking the sky among these trees of glass and steel are dozens of towering construction cranes.

I close my eyes, and search deep inside myself for that place where some things end and others begin. And, gazing into the darkness, try to find her there.

# Glitch

*Ed Wood*

This is a story that began one-hundred-and-fifty-million years ago. But for Richard Fisher, standing in his office, talking on his phone, looking out across the urban minarets of New York City, it began yesterday. "I'm really sorry, Mum. I'm not going to make it. I'm completely stuck." There was silence on the other end of the phone. He could feel the pain and disappointment seep through her.
"That's okay," she said, eventually.
"It's not okay. It's awful. I feel so..."
She cleared her throat: "Look, it can't be helped. Don't worry." She spoke without any emotion, without any inflection at all. "Perhaps you should have come last week."
"You told me not to; you told me everything was okay."
"I lied." The phone went dead.

Richard continued to hold the mobile to his ear, unable to believe or accept that the conversation had ended in such a way. Highly emotional, confrontation often left him on the verge of tears but this time he just felt numb. The phone on his desk rang and he picked it up, dropping the mobile into his shirt pocket. "Richard Fisher."

"It's me. Remember you have a video conference at eleven." Jayne's voice sounded pleasant and efficient, but, most of all, very familiar. "Are you okay?"

He thanked her and turned on the laptop, checking his mobile as he waited for start-up.

The conference lasted about thirty minutes. Richard couldn't really concentrate and there were connection problems which created an almost unmanageable drag. But he did gather that the exhibit, the installation that everyone wanted to see, was not going to be in his New York gallery by the weekend as promised; it was stuck in Paris; grounded by an ash cloud from a volcano that no one knew how to pronounce, let alone spell. He Googled it: *Eyjafjallajoekull*, according to the BBC on-line news, 'Island-Mountain-Glacier'.

The fallout from his missing exhibit would be considerable. Journalists, art critics and VIP guests would all have to be contacted, placated and reassured. But as he sat at his desk, staring at the computer screen, wondering about the exhibit – the cannon that splattered red paint against a wall, he decided that he couldn't care less. Everything he'd achieved, everything he'd strived for – all the sacrifices he'd made – had all been rendered meaningless by a volcano one-hundred-and-fifty-million years old.

Taking the slim, black mobile from his shirt pocket, he placed it on the desk next to his laptop; from his desk drawer, an MP3 player. On the far wall of the office there was a grey metal cabinet. Opening it, he took out a small lump-hammer. Holding the handle with his right hand, he allowed the dead-weight of it to drop into his left, gauging its suitability. Back at the desk, the hammer came down on the mobile phone first; as it disintegrated, the pieces bounced into the air then settled randomly around the point of impact.

The phone rang.

"It's me. I've just heard: they're allowing some flights in and out of Spain. Next one leaves in two hours."

"Can you--"

"I've already done it," Jayne said. "We leave in ten minutes."

Inspiration can arrive in the most unexpected circumstances. As Richard reached across for the photograph of his father, placing it into his briefcase, a still-life presented itself to him.

Richard had qualified with an MA in Fine Art many years earlier and was a painter of extraordinary talent, but after graduating, he'd become fascinated with modern art, particularly the work of the British artists Tracy Emin and Damien Hurst. After many unsuccessful attempts to join this new British movement, he had become a dealer, buying and selling the work of others. But with Hurst suing a seventeen year old art student for minor copyright infringements and Emin threatening a move to France to avoid paying high-rate tax on her multi-million pound fortune, the avant-garde had become the establishment and the mask of credibility had finally slipped to reveal the truth.

The smashed pieces of laptop, MP3 and mobile phone that littered Richard's desk looked exactly what they were. But placed in the pure-white space of his gallery and it was possible that he wouldn't need the cannon that splattered paint after all. He made a couple of phone calls and organised its installation at the gallery under the title of 'Glitch' – *an innovative and thought-provoking exploration into the limitations of information technology in the modern world.*

After a long flight to Spain and an even longer drive in a small hire-car to Paris, Richard and Jayne were finally heading back to London on the Eurostar. The fields passed by impassively and Richard took out the photograph from his briefcase: his father looked towards the camera, happy and giving a thumbs-up with his left hand. He wore a flat-cap and an oversized burgundy scarf tucked inside the front of his coat.
"I'd have never forgiven myself if I'd missed it," Richard said, looking up from the photograph.
Jayne replied pensively, "We're not there yet."
"I know, but..."
She let the magazine fall onto the table in front of her. "We'll make it. We haven't come all this way to miss it now." Richard was instantly reassured; his wife had that capability.
"Did you..." He hesitated. "Did you pack my black tie?"
She nodded. "You'd better ring your mum."
"I can't."
"Why not?"
Richard looked out of the window: in the fields there were lambs lazing around in the sunshine, squinting and flicking their tails to fend off the flies.

Cumulus clouds raked across the sky, their shadows playing across the hillsides. "Can I borrow your phone?" He asked finally.

## Lullaby : Barcarole

*Ke Huang*

A. birth : marriage

B. night : morning

C. cradle : gondola

D. song : poem

E. carol : sonneteer

 I knew I could say 'barcarole' in my head as to recall a similar-sounding Portuguese term, as the language's Latin roots came in handy when I tried to dissect obscure English words. Instead, the students with pale, brown, black skin bubbling their answer sheets around me turned to a blur and I only had eyes for the word 'lullaby.' I imagined I was a few months old, still living in China among parents and relatives, maybe wearing a fleecy tiger suit to scare off the bulging-eyed spirits. Grandmother would hold me in her arms, rocking me and chanting out a soft off-tune chant for her little pearl.

I had an urge to drop the pen and the pencil with the dull tip, rise from the hard chair and sprint out of the classroom of Grover Cleveland American School.

The amber streetlight shed a sparse gleam into the room, illuminating my hand-drawn poster with a table of all the world flags accompanied by captions of their names and capitals. The light even shaded the American flag with golden stars and its stripes resembled thin gold ingots.

On a Saturday, my routine was to wake up at eight, breakfast with my parents and accompany them to their clothing boutique in Restauradores. But that morning I had been awake since four, trying to fall asleep, convinced that staring at my alarm would help. Finally, the alarm turned 06:00. I read somewhere, or it could have been hearing from my brother, that Americans never have their hours digit any number higher than 12. After 12:59, their watches changed to 1:00PM. As much as I wished to go to college in America and learn about international diplomacy, I would never understand some of their customs. I knew that planning ahead could lead to disappointment; if all the colleges rejected me, my goals of living in New York City would vanish. Still, I imagined that if I was accepted to Columbia, I would live by the sister of my second uncle and that could teach me to understand them. Adapting to the States couldn't be as harsh cultural shock as when I came to Portugal from China -- all these chestnut brown-haired folks speaking their bitter language, their habit of walking dogs but not cleaning after, their obsession with red and green soccer teams. Little did I know that once I did come to America, I would miss Lisbon's temperate climate, the candid locals, intricate Manueline architecture and free public health care.

I heard a knock on the door. "Haizi." It irked me that ma still called me 'child' when I would turn eighteen in five months. I opened and saw her tousled boyish hair. She must have just woken up.

"Get ready while I make zaocan."

I didn't ask her if she needed help as my mission was to prepare for the SATs test site; it would start in fewer than three hours.

Looking inside my corduroy backpack, I fixed my eyes on the stripped HB pencil. The previous night, I crammed a leaf of a Continente ad with pencil lines to dull its dark grey tip; all to save time when I had to fill in the bubble sheet. While the students with sharp pencils colored their first bubble, as if filling a tank with a hose, my writing utensil poured out water at the rate of a wave. In my gingham case, next to the blunt pencil, I kept a pen. Being ambidextrous, I planned to hold it on my left hand and circle the question numbers I would leave for later.

The humming of the oil in the kitchen reminded me how the events in the previous two months enfolded opposite to what I expected. It wasn't ma who countered my plans to study international relations in America. Now I know what she implied to when telling me about the intentions of most of them, but at the time, all my frustration grew from how she would stop me from being alone with an elder man, Chinese or Portuguese. Not only merchants in the community, but even a male Portuguese sociology professor who accepted my application to intern as a research assistant. So, I was surprised with dad's response: "You want to go to America for college? You don't even know English."

"I always have twenties," the Portuguese equivalent to an A.

"Your brother's already there," he said driving ma and I to their shop facing the Restauradores Square's pencil-shaped marble obelisk.

"That's why I'm applying too." It occurred to me that I would be different; I was their daughter. As if it wasn't already unfair that he transferred Lanluo to Grover Cleveland American School beginning seventh grade where he received an intensive English education and I stayed at government-funded Nuno Golçalves (I could call myself lucky if my teachers only missed ten times a trimester). Now dad wanted to bar me from applying to American universities. As I needed his credit card to pay for college applications and admission tests, I needed his approval. The next day, after ma finished her morning prayer in her shrine gleaming with portly Buddhas and wired electric candles, I stopped by her and asked; but as I spoke, I became more convinced she would refuse to help me. What if she punished me for having the plan by sending me to a temple in China where I had to shave my head and take the vow of Buddhist nunnery?

"You can only apply to universities in New York," she answered. That was the city where our relative lived. I could tell her how it was unfair that Lanluo applied to schools around America but I acquiesced.

"I'll talk to your ba later."

When I ran back to the shop from school that afternoon, I couldn't be bothered holding up the flimsy Burberry-pattern fold-up umbrella and I let the drizzle nudge me. But I only found ma helping a customer with earrings the size of maple leaves.

"What did he say?" I asked, interrupting ma's pitch to the customer.

Like a traffic officer, she motioned for me to stop behind the counter. I complied and read the pages of *The Maias*, the Portuguese *Anna Karenina*, but instead of following the life and intrigues of the 19th century in Lisbon, I fretted about my life in the 21st.

As soon as the customer stepped out, I tried her again.

"Wait for dinner."

"If you think I shouldn't go, tell me."

"Don't be a sha haizi."

I waited for mother to take her seat while she stood by the sink and soaked her wok with water and detergent, she cooked her rich salmon and tofu soup and multicolored fried rice. When dad strode in and sat down, I was sure he knew. He glared at me and then turned to mother.

"Why do you want her to be too smart? She'll already have too much education if she goes to a university here."

"What do you mean 'too much education?' I won't spend a cêntimo of your precious money. I'll go if I get a scholarship. Without the test, they'll never know if I'm good enough." Ma tugged my sleeve as if pulling the blinds to shut my mouth. "It's not like I'm going to America to become a wanton woman. I want to learn about international politics and stop all the wars."

"Of course you do. All those politicians are waiting for you right now. They're telling themselves: 'Only if we have that daughter of those Chinese who own that shop in Portugal with us, all the wars and racism in the world will stop.' Don't you think I wasn't like you at your age? But there will always be shit in the world. Besides, you're a woman. No man wants a wife smarter than him."

"I don't need you to worry about who I'll marry. We're in the 21st century."

We finished the meal in silence.

While I was in the kitchen washing the dishes, dad slid under my door a slip of paper where he copied the numbers of his Visa card. The last time we talked was almost two months ago. For the first few weeks, every time he opened his mouth, I expected him to give in. Ma knew that she couldn't amend the fall out so she asked Lanluo.

"Apologize to ba," I heard him tell me as soon as mother pushed the phone handset to my ear.

"Hello to you too," the distance of the call made the phone echo my voice; it reminded me how the rest of the world heard me.

"You know him. He doesn't like to lose," you must mean he doesn't mind losing with you, his firstborn son.

Instead I said: "If there's nothing new with you, I have to go back and review some SAT lexicon," I handed the handset to ma. As I galloped to my room, I couldn't help to think if the feud between dad and I was only a contest. I wanted to hear him admit his mistake and be recognized as the winner.

I did the dishes of the breakfast while she went to pray at her shrine. I did consider joining her but since it'd be my debut prayer, I doubted it would work. If Guan Yin existed, She would deem my act as duplicitous. Let's punish the girl praying from Lisbon and make her score an 800. I speculated that praying for my own interest could turn into a case of, as the Portuguese say: *o feitiço vira contra to feiticeiro*, the curse turns against the wizard.

Heavy footsteps beat down the hall and kept soaping the bowl with the lemon-scented dish detergent. He must have realized I was right all along. I knew that wishing him to apologize would be like getting a 100 percentile, but at least he could be meeting me to wish me luck. Maybe he had changed his mind and would agree to drive me to Lanluo's old school. He stepped in and walked past me. I started to rinse the dishes. He must have opened the washing machine behind the dining table. He only comes in to stuff laundry? Only after he marched off did I realize that I was letting the water burn my hands. I turned off the faucet and noticed a blister on the side of my index finger; it glinted like a rough diamond.

Ma hurried in: "Are you okay? That was his way of wishing you luck."

"If he really wanted to, he would have opened his mouth and said it."

We descended the steep Angola Street, passing buildings coated with twill and arabesque-patterned tiles to head to Almirante Reis Avenue to where we expected to find cabs. Ma never learned to drive and I planned to start taking lessons that summer. After their liberal arts education, I envied the Americans for living in a country where they could learn to drive at the age of sixteen. Only talking to American friends in my freshman year, did I learn that the price of the low driving age were the fatal DUI accidents.

While waiting for the cab, ma forwarded me SAT words from the stack of cards I gave her. I had been ruminating on the words for months but some definitions still bemused me.

Since ma didn't know how to pronounce them, she had to spell them out. After my answer, she scrambled to decide if I was right; she would always end up pushing me the card.

A beige city taxi pulled in. I sat shogun because I would be directing the driver. Ma lived in Portugal three years longer than me but my language skills still exceeded hers, but what I topped her in Portuguese, she outdid me in Chinese. The worse was Lanluo, since he started to learn more English, he sounded even more awkward in Mandarin. After our first year in Portugal, when Lanluo and I spoke Chinese, we scattered a few words like *simpático* and *casaco*; once he started going to GCAS, he'd be tempted to scatter English words when talking to us, but as ma and ba didn't know the language, Lanluo'd have to stop the scattering and end up stuttering like an elementary school child with glossophobia. The same fate awaited me.

The cab radio played a sermon-sounding speech by the leader of the Popular Party. The driver, heavy and with sand-colored protruding teeth turned down the sound. He told me in Portuguese that ma and I were lucky because he was just about to end his shift. We offered him a smile, the kind we gave to an annoying relative. After asking a few questions about our trip and getting the clue we had no energy to make small talk, he turned up his radio.

Ma reached for her thin left wrist and removed her mahogany beaded Buddhist bracelet. I gestured her to resume the last minute SAT words quiz. She pushed at me the amulet and added: "It'll help you with the test."

I could have refused it and told her I believed in science, because religion limited free thinking; all her and the Chinese ladies from the Buddhist group escaped from facing real global inequalities by meeting every Sunday to chant lugubrious cryptic tunes.

Instead, I took the bracelet, wore it like a fancy wristwatch and thanked her.

When Lanluo was still a student, I had been to GCAS for a 4th of July barbecue. Dad drove us there while ma watched the shop. So, as the cab approached the campus, it occurred to me that it was her first time seeing the school.

"Lanluo never told me the buildings are only one-story tall."

Maybe she expected several high-tech edifices. The driver stopped the cab outside the school. I climbed out. Ma and I said bye in a way the Portuguese and Americans would call cold. Neither of us touched each other, but I felt ma's bracelet embracing my wrist.

"Call me when you finish," she said with a smiled hinting that she wished me to *chenggong*, succeed.

I raced to GCAS' main building but heard her call out; she reminded me to take the vocab cards. "You'll do well," she squeezed my hand like it was a chubby stress ball.

As I headed to the entrance, I flipped through the cards instinctively: 'inchoate -- adj. in an initial or

early state;' 'intransigent -- adj. stubborn; immovable; unwilling to change (n. intransigence)...'
"Are you Leo's sister?" Those were the first English words I heard a human say for a couple of weeks. The student referred to my brother by that alias because Lanluo named himself after Leonardo DaVinci (though I joked that he was the Chinese Leonardo DiCaprio, 'I'm the Emperor of the World!'). I lifted my head and saw a studious Portuguese boy of South Asian descent. Even after spending months studying English, I hesitated answering him in the language. I knew what 'panegyric' and 'perfidious' meant, but speaking it was another feat.

Aswayuja and I started talking and I learned that he knew Lanluo from playing soccer during lunch breaks. Then, my English was a mix of Chinese, Portuguese, British and American accents but I also knew self-consciousness was the biggest enemy of a language learner. Ma and her temple friends always said it was easier for us youngsters to acquire languages, but I believed that the main reason I picked up Portuguese and English was my confidence I would *chenggong*.

"Your English is pretty good."

I blushed at the idea that he could be flirting with me, but thankfully a handful of his classmates joined us. He introduced me to them but I had too many SAT words in my mind to remember their names.

A stalky American, the proctor, joined us. Aswayuja told me that normally the man wearing the blue shirt with a red C taught them P.E. I wanted to tell him that at Pedro Nunes the administration saved money by cutting the subject from our curriculum but the proctor was already requesting us to line outside the test room. He checked our passports and that was my first time seeing one issued by the United States. Unlike my burgundy-covered document bearing a seal of the Tiananmen Gate, five stars and a cheesy circular frame, the American navy blue jacket had a golden Zippo lighter censuring an eagle at the strategic spot.

I took a seat behind my new Indian friend. The proctor began to read the instructions. As I already knew them like the history behind the five permanent members of the Security Council, I zoned out to try to test myself on a few words, instead, I surveyed the room and got distracted with trying to identify the portraits that hung around the walls. The only one I recognized was thin-lipped George Washington. I couldn't take my eyes off a familiar-looking younger man with puffy eyes and fleshy lips. I remember seeing him before but always with his elegant small-faced wife who wore a pink suit and a hat shaped like a cake. Compared to the other men, he had to be the handsomest.

The proctor handed us the SAT packet and it must have taken us half an hour to fill its cover sheet. It wasn't that I didn't understand him, but as he talked with his American accent, I imagined that I was at home watching Sabrina, the Teenage Witch. Unlike the program on RTP 2, what he said wasn't accompanied by Portuguese subtitles. I had heard teachers speaking the language before, but the English teachers at ESPN (Escola Secundária de Pedro Nunes, that is) were trained in England, they always sounded surprised and never pronounced Ts as Ds. As I bubbled L-A-N-... I became conscious I was locked in a room like that in an alien universe. I asked what I was doing there. Which school would give me a scholarship? What if all these months of studying left nothing in my head, like a balloon being popped by a sharp pencil lead?

"You have twenty-five minutes for this section," he said a few more words but I couldn't decipher them. It was as if an invisible tent surrounded me. I opened the booklet to the right page, only to stare at the question. I told myself I had plenty of choices. I could guess or leave it blank and return to it later, but staring at the question would only be a waste of time. With the dull pencil pressed against my blister, I chided myself for not doing anything for my ticket to America when I gave up hours of going out with friends to practice SAT questions. Every time a neighboring student's watch ticked, I felt my score plummeting. Back in my head, I heard dad's voice telling me that I shouldn't be sitting there. I would be wiser spending my time applying to Portuguese universities. Stop being a monkey trying to grasp the moon.

I scanned the students around me; even with their sharp pencil points, they sped down the questions. Some flipped the page of the test book. I took a gander at the portraits along the wall and remembered the name of the handsome and confident man. He guided American astronauts to the moon. Maybe the destination the monkey pursued was an attainable goal.

Ba's voice stopped. I looked down at the test, started it and only guessed blindly one question for that section. The dull pencil came in handy and, as a full-blooded Chinese, I breezed through the math section. For the break, I sat with my fellow test-takers and chatted and they found my educational background intriguing. Maybe I would fit in with Americans after all. We then compared some answers and I found I didn't make too many mistakes. Instead of blaming myself for having blocked earlier, I commended myself for the questions I answered correctly.

The difficulty of the next sections increased but I only paused thrice. One even tested a word ma had asked me earlier: 'saturnine.' Before I knew, the proctor called out time over. I meant to call ma immediately but Aswayuja and I were talking again.

"Do you remember Leo's prom?" How couldn't I? It was all he talked about for a whole trimester. Aswayuja and I headed toward the entrance. His classmates whispered among themselves. I was only wearing jeans and a made in China nonsensical-phrased sweatshirt. He couldn't have that in mind. "If you're not busy that night, I thought you may want to, you can say no if you don't want to, you know, go with me. If you're not busy."

It took me a few seconds to understand what he said, but once I got it, I let out a chuckle and nodded: "I'd love to!"

As we stepped out, we exchanged numbers. I didn't feel like a tramp because I told myself that Aswayuja knew Lanluo and wasn't a stranger ma liked to warn me about.

We parted and he went to his parent's Volkswagen. I pressed my phone off the address book and dialled for ma, I heard a vehicle honking. I recognized the Mercedes down the street and rubbed my eyes to ensure that the driver I saw inside was who I secretly wished it was.

# The Country Club

*J F Chavoor*

Teachers get forty minutes at lunch. That's five minutes to get to the lunchroom, five minutes standing in line which leaves you with half an hour. I know one year they gave us thirty minutes at lunch, leaving us twenty minutes to dine and socialize. So when we have institute days, which are nonstudent days featuring seven hours of meetings, we like getting a whole hour for lunch. Many teachers are very creative with their sixty minutes. They know that the administrators in charge won't roll up until at least the seventieth minute and that people will mill around for another five minutes after that which leaves late comers with an eighty minute lunch. Now with eighty minutes you can actually go to a nearby restaurant and not have to rush. There is no dawdling though. You have to have already asked a few friends where they're heading before lunch starts and then you have to head straight to your car and go. If you don't plan ahead you might end up eating where you didn't want to or with people you hadn't planned on hanging out with at lunch. Or you might end up eating lunch alone until you spotted someone you knew only tangentially.

I don't know how I missed connections with my friends that day but I ended up at my car alone with no plan and no idea who was going where. I guessed that some of them might go to Javier's, a popular Mexican restaurant only a couple of miles from Roosevelt. There was a place closer to school, El Sombrero, but the food there was old and stale, served warm not hot. The ambience was worn, torn and faded. It was the kind of place you would only go if you had been going there for years and years and now you just couldn't give up on the relationship; after all those years it had become a matter of loyalty.

I could have driven by El Sombrero's first but I didn't. I didn't want to eat at a place that was a distant second to Javier's even if my good friends were there. I made myself believe that they had chosen Javier's as I headed up Kings Canyon Avenue.

None of my colleagues were there. There was a good noontime crowd but even after I surveyed the place front to back, side to side there were no Roosevelt peers to be seen. The clock was running and I was hungry so I decided I would eat there alone and go back to the dull meetings with that full, sleepy feeling. I would even buy myself an after dinner mint. I was being escorted to my seat when I saw Aram. I wasn't sure at first but as I passed his booth we glanced at each other but didn't speak.

I knew him and he knew me but ours was an unusual history: fifty years earlier he had dated Mom. I also had been on good terms with his daughter since meeting her seventeen years earlier at an Armenian Christian

Endeavour Union retreat where she was the keynote speaker. I liked what she had to say at the time and I liked her calm, occasionally droll speaking style. It was as if she could understand things and help others understand things by slowing everything down, and it was a time when everyone was anxious to speed things up. Debra's approach was a gift few people possess.

But in the moment, we were two men, a thirty-four year old English teacher and a seventy-four year old retired chemist. I thought about going over to his booth to say hi and possibly join him for lunch but I worried that we wouldn't have much to say to each other, and besides maybe he was waiting for a friend which would serve only to underscore my eating alone, which in my mind was second only to going to the movies alone under the category of social oddness. I felt obliged to at least say hello. I got up and walked back to where he was.

"Oh hi," I said cheerily, as if I had seen him for the first time.

"Hi," he said, "what're you doing eating alone?"

"I don't know," I answered, unable to think of anything, "I just, it was lunch time and I..."

"Wanna come over here?"

"Oh, yeah sure." The waitress handed me a menu without comment.

"You like this place?"

"Yeah. We come here a lot."

"Huh."

"You?"

"It's all right."

He seemed distracted. I didn't want to ask why he was eating lunch alone. His countenance was stern; he looked like Winston Churchill in one of those pictures where he appeared to be considering weighty matters.

"How long've you been in Fresno?" he asked after I ordered.

"Almost ten years."

"Like it?"

"Yeah. I like the affordable housing. Coming from LA."

"Huh."

"I mean what do you with your social time? You have someone over or you go over to someone's house. You go to the movies. You can do that here as well as anywhere."

"Fresno's not like it was."

"Yeah." I thought he meant it wasn't as good as it once was.

"There was a lot of prejudice against Armenians."

"I've heard about that."

"I was a good athlete when I was in high school."

"I played football in high school," I said, not sure why he suddenly jumped subjects.

"I was good at football and track."

"Never liked track. Running any distance was like torture to me."

"I was good at sprints. I ran for the JV squad."

"Yeah?"

"I ran better than the kid who ran varsity. Understand?"

"Better?"

"Better times. Record times."

"But...."

"Know what the track coach said to me?"

"No."

"He didn't want an Armenian doing better than a white kid."

"What?"

"That's why he kept me on JV." His face and the tone of his voice indicated that the incident was still causing him pain.

"You gotta be kidding."

"That's what he said. That's exactly what he said."

I had heard stories. Uncle Harry, Mom's brother served in World War II, came home and couldn't find a job; they weren't hiring Armenians in Fresno. According to the story, Dad suggested that Uncle Harry put on his uniform and go back to the dozen or so places where he had been told that he—as an Armenian—was automatically disqualified for consideration and stand before the employer and ask, "Now what am I?"

Armenians, African Americans and Mexican Americans could not buy property on the exclusive Huntington Boulevard; neither could they join the country club. We were even assigned our very own pejorative label, "Fresno Indians." I didn't bring up Uncle Harry or anyone else on Mom's side of the family though; I didn't want him to think that I was going to try to draw him out on the subject of him and Mom.

Mom told me the story when I was in high school one rainy day while she made dinner preparations. She had dated him. She went to Fresno State while he attended Cal Berkeley. She had a job at her uncle's hamburger place across the street from Fresno High, and she used some of her money to send to him. Now, according to Mom—and it is freely admitted that Mom would not be an unbiased source—she went one day to meet him at the train depot and he got off the train with his finance. This, according to Mom, after six years as his "steady girl." She told the story without any animosity, and she didn't describe anything past that moment when Aram stepped off the train. We simply listened to the rain drumming on the kitchen window and then she put the pot roast in the oven. She never brought the subject of Aram up again.

Ten years after she told me the story I met Aram for the first time. It was the Fresno High School 50th Class Reunion at the bar at Cedar Lanes Bowling alley. There were about twenty-five alumni in attendance and someone took roll which turned into toll accounting.

"Floyd Johnston?"

"He's dead."

"Bernice Thompson?"

"Alzheimer's. Doesn't recognize her own kids."

There was a kind of grim humor and nonchalance to the whole procedure as the man in the front taking roll would draw a line through the name of the newly discovered dead or disabled.

Aram was near the front; Mom and I arrived late and hung in the back while she looked for familiar faces. Between sips of gin and tonic, I wondered if she would make her way up front and what she might say to her former beau from forty-five years ago.

"Come on," she said like a hunter who had spotted a well-hidden prey.

I debated whether to put my drink down where we were or take it with me and she got ahead of me. I worked my way around men who were recalling fifty year old football games as if they had just happened that week, manoeuvred past women who were trying to figure out if they knew each other back when, and finally almost bumped into Mom when she stopped suddenly where Aram was sitting.

"Hey," she said.

"Hey, kid," he replied. They stood eyeing each other wordlessly for a beat, then Mom turned, apparently satisfied with this exchange, and we went back to our original spot. They didn't speak to each other the rest of the night, and I don't think I saw him again until we had lunch together at Javier's.

"Prejudice against Armenians?" I said, to see if he had any more experiences to share.
"It was like a country club."
"Yeah, Armenians couldn't get in to the...."
"No, that's not what I'm talking about. The coaches, the school, the college, everything. It was all like a country club. Armenians weren't invited."
"Oh, yeah."
"I was good in sports. They had no reason to keep me on JV." It still had power; he appeared to be freshly enraged.

When our food arrived we ate with vigor. We kept moving the conversation from one topic to another. He was clearly intelligent and articulate. I couldn't help comparing him with Dad. It seemed that Mom's paradigm for boyfriends did not change much. Both men had a clear sense of right and wrong and had expectations for everyone to uphold those ideals. They also had remarkable long-term memory capacity.

I drove back to Roosevelt in a starch induced daze. I thought about the all the Armenian names I had seen flipping though old Roosevelt yearbooks: Abajian; Hanoian; Manoogian; Garabedian. Had any of them been discriminated against? According to what I heard from the older teachers, Roosevelt and the Sunnyside area was awash in Armenians. I imagined it would be nice to attend a public school with my fellow Armenians. At Burroughs High, my high school, there were four of us: Mike Ezmerlian; Mike Delbarian; Virginia Frankian; and Chavoor. Maybe no one bothered us because they didn't know we existed. I pulled into the parking lot thinking I should have asked Frankian to the prom, among other cloudy, far away thoughts.

I went to the English department meeting exactly fifteen minutes late, sat in the back of the room. I was thinking about Kathleen, my three year old, wondering what kind of town Fresno would be for her or if she would ever encounter any kind of exclusion for any reason. I thought about Mom who experienced a different but no less damaging kind of exclusion. Would she have gone to college at all if it were not across the street from their house? Would she have stayed in college long enough to graduate if she weren't waiting for Aram to finish at Berkeley? And might it have been said that I was following my mother's footsteps if she had become an English teacher instead of a homemaker as prescribed by the era? It seemed that Aram and Mom were both victims of the same country club.

The department chair went on and on about literature based instruction, unaware of all the other issues moving around in my head like a hypnotist's watch. I closed my eyes and started to doze when a colleague leaned over and asked me where I went for lunch.

"I met an old friend at Javier's." He nodded and I leaned back, laced my fingers together, set them on my contented stomach and nodded off.

# Embroidering

*Viccy Adams*

The security camera makes short, jerky movements as it scans the room. The receptionist is watching him watching it watching him. It has crossed his mind that this might prove to be the initial stage of assessment, an unmentioned part of the review of his personality. He keeps his face dispassionate. When the camera pauses in his direction he meets its blank gaze and imagines he is making eye contact with whoever is checking the screen in the back room. There is no need to smile, so he doesn't. Eye contact can be a powerful weapon, especially in a war of this kind. Against the world. One of his contacts is slipping, a faint irritation to the side of his eye. Brown over brown, just the smallest difference he could find between his iris and the colour the package promised. He has twenty-twenty vision, these are cosmetic only. He isn't supposed to wear them every day, but he doesn't normally go out every day. This week is proving to be an exception and his eyes are rebelling a little; inflaming slightly and this contact keeps trying to migrate. He can twitch it back into place easily enough, but wants to wait until the camera has changed direction. There -- an opportunity taken.

They make his eyes slightly void of expression, harder to read. His hair matches; made uniform. He is erasing traces of his personality systematically. Secretly. Nobody knows he has the contacts. Nobody knows he dyes his hair. They know he takes ages in the bathroom, washes his own towels. He cleans the place thoroughly each time, through the haze of steam, then puts the empty dye packets inside a bag inside a bag inside a bag in the bin in his room. Which he empties himself, once a week, on bin day. His hair hangs heavily over his neck. Not hippy long, just in continual need of a cut to neaten it up. It hangs over the tattoo that nobody knows about. One thick black line half an inch under the hair line. No colour, no words, no pattern. It is there simply to prove a point. Same as him.

The room is as much of a blank canvas as he is. Pure white, minimalist. The receptionist is moving piles of paper around on top of the counter, her white uniform contrasting with the white of the counter, with the white of the documents she displaces, with the white of the seat he is waiting on. The lights must be kept this dim to stop clients being dazzled he thinks. He is dressed in shades of grey. Black would be too much of a statement. He is not some teenage Goth utterly lacking in imagination. They are trying to be impressive, it must take a lot of effort to keep it looking this clean and fresh. White is clinical and probably calming. They are trying to neutralise his emotions. He is one step ahead of them there. No angry teen music. No music at all, actually. If he listened to music they would use it as a clue. No music, no posters in his room. Doesn't read anything except school books and whatever is given to him for a present at Christmas or for a birthday. Polite but not forthcoming. Like the receptionist. She is impressive. Very white teeth. Welcoming smile without a hint of compliance or caring. Part of the very white, very crisp uniform. She hasn't even been looking at him out of interest. It seems she looks at everything in the room periodically, checking it is still in its allotted place.

It is warm in here. He never rolls up the sleeves of his shirt. Not even in high summer. It would look too casual is one thing, but also then they would see the piercings in his wrists. An inch back from the bony bits which stick up where his hand rotates from. Long surface piercings that his body is still struggling to reject, despite the rigid schedule of cleaning. They will heal properly, given time. One on each side; symmetrical. Plain grey to match the rest of his outfits. The main thing is to keep them unexpected. To keep himself unexceptional in presentation. He had wanted to get his bellybutton pierced, but it had seemed a bit trite. Too obvious. These were much better. Hardcore. He paints his toenails sometimes, but not at the moment. It was starting to get a bit hackneyed. There was also the concern that the blood-red might show through his socks, were he to take his shoes off. He hasn't found anything to replace the painting. That irritates him; a part of his secret life is missing. Perhaps a toe-ring. Worn on a different toe each day to signal to himself what he is really feeling. To show that he is angry, lonely, unhappy on the left foot. Five toes. He needs two more emotions. But it wouldn't fit the big toe. And it might fall off the little toe. One ring can't fit all the different shapes and sizes. So keep it to three options. Then for the right foot, three more. Three emotions for good days. Smug, satisfied, ecstatic? They are for moments, not a whole day. He can't be bothered with having to move it from toe to toe continually. Bored, tired, miserable. Maybe not a toe-ring. Maybe he will go back to painting his toenails. Yes. But with clear nail varnish. Thus displaying the utter pointlessness of the action; all about the doing and not the result. The means and not the end. Perfect.

He had made one mistake. One small gesture of cynicism, and here he was. Art class. Art and Design Technology. He should have stuck to the rules. His rules. The establishment was not supposed to be aware that he was sticking his middle finger up at them. An unexpected mistake. He hadn't even realised that they had called his parents until the knock on the classroom door and he was called to the office. There both of them were, together again. United in his defeat. So, so terribly concerned and so, so terribly worried. Pathetic. But, of course, it is all fine because the most expensive psychiatrist in town just happens to have an appointment available this week. Rushed here before he has a proper amount of time to think. He will be expected to talk about it to this stranger who, he assumes based on their taste in interior décor, will most certainly be wearing a white coat. And, of course, they feel so, so terribly disappointed in themselves. Hushed words. The divorce, of course. But he had seemed to be coping so well. Such a nice boy. Thank you so much for letting us know. How are his grades? Average? Good, good, no change there. Exactly average? As if he had studied the statistics and set out to achieve absolute mediocrity? But they didn't pick up on that. They weren't supposed to. This sudden outburst of creativity? Not from my side, not from my side. Perhaps one of the teachers is a bad influence. No, not here in this school. He hadn't actually been asked any questions directly. Nobody had even asked him why. He had just sat there and witnessed the hurried interchanges between his parents. Both of them, same room, same time. And the qualifying comments from the headmistress. Anxious to avoid losing a set of fees. Driving home (best he takes a couple of days off) they had sat in the usual silence. So, so civilised.

The receptionist coughs quietly, clearing her throat. He looks in her direction again, but she is only preparing to make a phone call. He can hear each tap of her fingernails as she dials, but then she turns her chair a little and he can't lip read, and can't make out the words without studying her face because her voice is a low, soft purr. Just a short phone call. Probably confirming an appointment. Something like that. The security camera moves past him again, pauses to observe the other corner of the room. He hasn't discovered a pattern to the pauses and the jerks. Not yet. If he has to come back again he will be able to make a comparison with the patterns. He will have to note it down in his head for the moment. It would be too obvious if he wrote it down while he was here. If he is under observation then they would want to know what he was doing and why. The fewer starting points he gives them, the better. He had rather enjoyed it, the miniature rebellion. The results, not so good. Being noticed, not so good. Being here, not so good. Presumably everything was going to have to change from now on. Unless he could be so utterly convincing that they thought there had been some mistake. Some small aberration. An explainable blip on the radar. He was good at helping them smooth everything over.

The assignment had been in textiles. The idea had come to him, and he hadn't been able to resist it. It was an out-of-hours piece, or he would not have been able to pull it off. They were given the materials, and the long holiday weekend. He had stopped at the corner shop on the way home, bought the rest of what he needed. The banana had been easiest; such pliable skin. The needle had gone through easily, no problems with tearing. The apples were the worst. Under-ripe. Difficult to stop the thread from pulling through. It had taken several attempts, several discarded to the snack pile. But he was pleased with the finished result, with the shading of colours over the contours. The grapes took ages because they were so small. The juices ran everywhere and soaked the thread, but that was pretty much what he had expected. He had done them individually, tying them back onto the stalk each in turn. It was ambitious, but he had reined himself in, stuck with just the three types of fruit. It was all the colour contrast he had needed. Plus, he didn't have the right coloured thread for the couple of kiwis he had briefly considered adding. Didn't want to raise suspicions anyway. Then when it was finished he had washed most of the stickiness from his hands and spent the remainder of the final afternoon arranging them in the bowl. He had checked twice, and he had followed the assignment to the letter. Class, we will be studying still-life this term. Embroider a bowl of fruit.

The camera is staring directly at him again. Without meaning to, he has started smiling. The receptionist is watching him too. He freezes his expression, tries to make it into a look of absent contentment and pleasure. He doesn't know where to look. Call their bluff. Look into the camera, look away again. Pretend not to have noticed. Look at the receptionist. Look just past her head. Let the smile fade back into obscurity. Make a mental note, does the camera look in the same direction as the receptionist? He'd like to check his watch, but it feels too soon. He doesn't want to be seen to be doing too much at once. This waiting feels like an interrogation. He thinks they might be breaking him. Cracking under the pressure. Another half hour and all they will have to do is ask one question and everything will unstitch and come pouring out. He needs to pull himself together, find the strength to carry on. Carry on just as normal.

# Girl on a Street Corner

*Vivienne McCulloch*

She stood on the corner, her face showing pale under the streetlamp. I was on my way to bed, laptop turned off, mug and book in hand when I noticed her from my second-floor window. It was the first time I'd seen a hooker in my street. I was intrigued enough to turn off the light, go through and switch on my bedside lamp then slip back to look at her from my chair in the darkened lounge.

At least, I was assuming she was a hooker. Now that I was making a point of studying her, she looked to me far prettier and healthier than any I'd seen. Her hair was well-cut, falling in thick, soft waves to her shoulders. Blonde, but either it was naturally so or expensively dyed for there was none of the harshness that comes out of a drugstore bottle. She was tall and slender, and both her poise and movement suggested that she was very fit.

Perhaps she wasn't waiting for business after all, but for a friend or a lover. On the other hand, she was dressed in a tightly-belted leather coat, fish-nets and stilettos. No hint of shirt or dress showed at the neck of the coat; there might be nothing but underwear beneath the soft leather. Or nothing at all. I shifted slightly in my seat at the thought. As I did so, the girl lifted her head as if listening, then moved away from the brick wall with a swift grace that was almost shocking. Now she leant on the lamppost in a timeless pose. Her left knee thrust out, she curled one arm around the metal behind her. Chin up; she looked down the street from under her lashes. I contemplated lighting a cigarette, but I didn't want to move. I had the uncanny feeling that she knew I was watching her.

The sound of a car coming down the street dispelled the feeling, so I took the opportunity to move to the other side of the window to get an earlier sight of it. It was just an ordinary family sedan. It slowed down and rolled to a halt by the girl. The driver stuck his head out of the window and said something. She unpeeled herself from the streetlamp, bending cat-like to reply. Whatever the guy had said, she apparently wasn't interested. With a shake of her hair, she stood up, resuming her seductive pose. The driver appeared to hesitate for a moment, and then he got out and locked the car. The girl smiled at him. It wasn't the whiteness of her teeth or the beautiful curves of her mouth that made her smile so mesmerising. It was some other quality altogether. A quality that made my mouth open and my cheeks burn; that rocked me back on my heels; that made me hate the thirty-something redneck glued to the sidewalk in front of her.

The girl took his arm and guided him around the corner into the darkness. I returned to my seat on weakened legs and lit a cigarette. I'd forgotten whether to be glad or sorry that she turned out to be a hooker after all. I was trembling. I don't know for how long I sat there, other than it was long enough to smoke three cigarettes, one after the other. She reappeared so quickly I almost missed her. She was alone. She took car keys from her pocket and unlocked the door of the sedan. One hand on the door, she paused. I held my breath. Slowly, she raised her head and looked up to my window. Somehow she saw through the darkness of the room. She looked right into my eyes. I still wasn't breathing. I felt that neither was she. Her upturned face was perfect. She dropped her gaze. I exhaled. Then she got into the car and drove away.

# Jam Tomorrow

*Abi Wyatt*

There's something satisfying about making a nice jam, especially when you have grown and gathered all the fruit yourself. Sometimes, that's not possible, of course, not in this day and age. Gardens are so much smaller now, hardly big enough for a decent-sized shrub, never mind a fruit-bearing tree. But there are ways around obstacles like this, ways of making the best of things; little compromises and wrinkles that you learn over time. I like to get my strawberries, for instance, from the 'Pick Your Own' down the road, and Mrs D. from next door but one is happy to exchange her excess blackberries for a pot or two of home-made jam 'without all the mess.' Best of all, though, is the blackberries that grow hereabouts; the hedgerows are fairly overloaded with them - and I usually chop up a couple of nice Bramleys, shop-bought if needs be. There's very little pectin in blackberries and jam won't thicken without it. You can buy pectin but I prefer not to do so. I'm partial to some blackberry and apple, especially on a home-made scone.

A friend of mine – well, more of an acquaintance, really – once looked down her nose and said you could just as easy buy it from the supermarket and it wasn't worth the fuss.

"Fuss," I said to her, "but that's the fun of it."

Well, it is, isn't it? First, you've got to locate your jars and then you've got to wash and dry them. There's a lot of pleasure to be had just from seeing them ready to use, all lined up and sparkling in the sun. Then you've got to pick over your fruit and make sure it's clean. With soft fruit like blackcurrants and gooseberries, I like to leave it to soak. Then, I'll rinse and dry my stainless steel pan – it gets that dusty in that bottom cupboard – and I lay out my ladle, my thermometer and, of course, my wooden spoon. Myself, I like a proper wooden spoon, though opinions do differ. I know they stain but, to my way of thinking, a wooden spoon is essential.

I said as much to Dr Rahoud last time I was there. I had taken him two two-pound jars of the damson and apple. – Well, I had so much, you see, more than Clive and I could ever hope to eat – and I'd already given to the Hospice stall at our annual Harvest Fayre.

"Mrs Frost," he said, "I have no doubt but that you are right. On such a matter, you are, and must remain, the undisputed authority."

Now wasn't that nice of him? Such lovely manners. His skin in the colour of milky coffee and he's got these beautiful eyes; really thick lashes, much thicker than I've seen on any girl. Sometimes, when he's taking to me, I lose track of what he's saying because all I can think of is these chocolate eyes. Anyway, when I gave him this jam, he came over quite emotional; kept on repeating, over and over, that he didn't know what to say.

Eventually, though, he pulled himself together and we got down to business.

"How have you been feeling since we met last time?" He generally starts off like that. I think he thinks it eases me into it. "How is Mr Frost? Busy in the garden, I expect."

He will insist on dragging Clive into it. It's the one thing that irritates me about our little chats. I don't go there to talk about Clive. It's got nothing whatsoever to do with him. Clive is never in the house when they come. They come to see me.

"Mr Frost has been out a lot. I've hardly had reason to speak to him." I snapped a bit so that he would know not to mention Clive again. I had my handbag on my knee so I rummaged around pretending to look for a tissue. Dr Rahoud soon got the hint. He's very sharp like that. He asked about the headaches and whether they were better or worse. I told him they were about the same and that maybe I needed new glasses.

"No," he said, "no, no. I don't think that will make a great difference."

Then he smiled a kind of dreamy smile and everything went back to normal. He had something to write down and we both began to relax.

I've been seeing Dr Rahoud for several months. It's worked out better than I thought. Of course, I was quite suspicious at first. I expected him to be like the rest of them, full of questions but over-friendly and always faintly sneering. Everything they said made you more and more certain they were trying to catch you out. It's true he did ask a lot of questions; but when someone's polite and interested, well, you don't mind that, do you? Soon, I was looking forward to seeing him; it made me feel – understood. Nowadays I tend to make it an outing of it; afterwards, I pop into town after and pick up a few odds and ends. There's a very smart little cafe I've found that serves wonderful cake. I shouldn't be eating cake, I know, but it's my little indulgence. Clive won't go in there at all; he says it's over-priced.

Anyway, where was I? That's right, Dr Rahoud. When he'd finished writing, he flicked back through his notes and gave a little nod.

"Tell me, Mrs Frost, have you had a – visit since your last appointment? If you have, perhaps you'd like to tell me all about it."

Well, as it happened, I had had a visit, just three days before. But I didn't like the way he hesitated; it put my back right up. For that split second, he sounded like them, as though he was talking to a schoolgirl.

"No," I said, "I haven't seen them lately. The last time was more than a month ago. I told you all about it. I told you last time."

He flicked back in his notes again and I waited while he read them. There were two little lines between his eyebrows that showed that he was thinking hard.

"Ah, yes," he said. He picked up his pen and twiddled it between his thumb and forefinger. "I remember, Mrs Frost, that, on this occasion, you experienced considerable distress. I have a note here" – and he read aloud as though he was impatient to finish – "You were rendered powerless by some form of hypnosis and, very much against your will, you were subjected to a whole series of investigative procedures. And it was after that that the Tall Grey Doctor carried out the mind-scan? He leaned down over you and stared into your eyes? Have I got that right?"

It was at this point that I began to feel a bit upset. It wasn't that the notes were wrong but he was making what I told him sound silly. I tried to pull my thoughts into the shape of sentences but the words just slipped away.

I said: "He made me feel things in my body that I didn't want to feel."

Dr Rahoud realised that something was wrong. He put down his pen and put his fingertips together to make a kind of steeple. Then he looked at me with his huge, caramel eyes. There was a long pause before he smiled and his tone was almost tender. "Mrs Frost," he said, "how would you describe your relationship with your husband?"

Do you know that expression 'a red mist came down'? Well, I used not to understand quite what it meant. I understand now, though, because it came down then. I had in my head no other thought but to kill him. I wanted to thrust my hand into his chest and drag out his startled heart. I didn't, though; somehow, I managed to struggle to my feet. Then I actually walked to the door where I turned and looked at him. His eyes weren't so beautiful, after all; in fact, he looked quite ordinary.

"I've told you," I hissed at him, "they come to see me. Clive has nothing to do with it. And, Dr Rahoud, make no mistake, there'll be no more damson jam."

# Apocalypso

*John Rachel*

The guy was ubiquitous.

Recently, Billy had been seeing Apocalypso posters everywhere, some with catchy sayings, some announcing prayer meetings and rallies. He even spotted a small billboard in China Town, written in Chinese characters no less. The guy had his own Public Access TV show. And though Billy didn't bother to read it, he saw a feature article on him in the Village Voice, titled "Guru To The Moral Minority".

Billy finally succumbed to what increasingly appeared to be inevitable.

He was going to go to an Apocalypso function.

Candy was into it. She would be __ quirky as she was ninety-nine per cent of the time.

"This must be the place."

"So right you are."

Billy and Candy had just made the short walk from the subway station to a former bank building in Tribeca which was rented out for performance art events, concerts and parties.

"You know, I've known about this guy for some time now. His headquarters, the Ashram of the Urban Night, is right near my place. Right on 1st Avenue."

"I can't believe you've been keeping this from me, Billy."

"After this evening, you might wish I had."

As they approached the building, they could hear over loudspeakers what sounded like heavy male monk voices in a rhythmic incantation.

YO - HAMA - HAMA - YAMA - YO
YO - HAMA - HAMA - YAMA - YO
YO - HAMA - HAMA - YAMA - YO
YO - HAMA - HAMA - YAMA - YO

They paid the admission and went inside.

The "temple" was so crowded with chanting, dancing, rapturous bodies, apparently at the peak of spiritual merriment, it was nearly impossible for Billy to squeeze into the main hall. With Candy in tow, he used his scrum legs and moshpit skills to best advantage, grunting and hurling forward into the tumbling sea of enlightenment seekers, incurring more than once the disdain of someone he had shoved aside with his unenlightened aggressiveness.

As they entered the cavernous main hall, they were assaulted by dazzling display of intense multi-colored lights and a thunderous explosion of sound.

boompa - ta-ta-ta-ta-ta-ta boompa - ta-ta
boompa - ta-ta
boompa - ta-ta-ta-ta-ta-ta boompa - ta-ta
boompa - ta-ta

Four drummers __ bare from the waste up but adorned with Chinese jute hair ties and necklaces of teeth, bones, shells and flowers __ thrashed out a driving, infectious rhythm on two sets of congas, prayer bells, a tabla and a djembe. The two conga players were the dark chocolate of the Congo, smooth and taught in their youthful muscularity. Their shiny oiled cornrows spawned long braids which thrashed and bounced about in sync with their histrionic hand chops to the drums. The djembe player was albino but he had shaved his head and eyebrows, and applied red and black war paint to his face and torso.

He was always laughing at some musical joke only he could hear, and regularly made eye contact either with the other percussionists or members of the audience, encouraging them to laugh along. The man on the prayer bells and tabla was actually a woman, but one who had played down her femininity to the point where her gender was not so much of an issue as was her species. Her tangled, unwashed hair dragged across her snarling face, sticking to her cheeks. She held her mouth open wide and clicked her teeth together in time with the music, creating the impression she was trying to snatch insects out of the air. She was wearing huge farmers' overalls and no shirt, offering glimpses nobody wanted, of the flabby udders on her chest. Whenever she played the prayer bells, her eyes rolled back in her head suggesting the urgent need for an exorcism.

Competing for the audience's eye with this malformed menagerie of musicians, were several spontaneous dancers who either possessed by the rhythms or a need for attention, had jumped onstage and were whirling about in a freeform frenzy of euphoria. First there were two, three, then finally four girls, egging one another on to greater heights of improvised showmanship. The floor around them was wet with their perspiration, and their pheromones filled the air.

People watched the drummers and go-go girls, slackjawed by the visuals and riveted by the sonics, for thirty minutes before the star of this evening's performance made his appearance. Once Apocalypso took the stage, all eyes fixed on him.

It was no celebrity walkway entrance. Dressed in nothing but a simple white sarong, hair pulled back off of his face in long dreadlocks and tied into a single clump in back, no facial hair other than thick eyebrows which set off his intense brown eyes, handsome to the point of causing gasps from the females __ and of course the gay men __ in any room he entered, medium height but muscular and thick with lean masculinity, Apocalypso stepped easily and gracefully onto the stage.

"It is my honor to be here with you, to feel and absorb and radiate with you the energy of our shared divinity. We are here to begin a new beginning. A new beginning for each of us here. A new beginning for the spiritually empty people of the nation which once held great promise. A new beginning for America. A new beginning for the world. Into the great void __ the gaping chasm left by the empty pursuit of material wealth, the emptying of all value from the human mind by modern media, into the desolate vacuum the banks and corporations have thrust the souls of good people like ourselves to gasp and face extinction __ into that artificially-created black hole of nothingness, we send our infinite love and the boundless energy of our shared enlightenment. We each are one of many. We are a many of ones. But our singularity is an illusion. For all is but the Oneness of All. Let us now commune in silence and let the power of our Oneness flood the world with the majesty of our love."

The entire audience __ there must have been over two thousand people crowded into the building __ stopped talking, stopped moving, stopped breathing. The only sounds that could be heard were those bleeding through the thick bank walls from the street.

After about a minute, Apocalypso raised his hands heavenwards as if to invite the approval of invisible onlooking deities. He then lowered his arms and let them hang at his side. With an impish grin, he shrugged his shoulders, smiled broadly showing the full splendor of his white even teeth, then walked off the stage as calmly as he had come on only minutes before.

The crowd went wild, the drummers again started pounding away, and the party to celebrate the coming spiritual revolution was underway again.

Behind all of the flowery, high-sounding phrases and painful mix of metaphors, there really wasn't much message to Apocalypso's message.

It wasn't the words that moved people.

It was the man.

Whether he consciously knew this, or was guided by the gift of solid instincts, Apocalypso used his effect on people to his fullest advantage. He took them where he wanted them to go. He got them to do what he wanted them to do.

There were naturally a few hard-core naysayers and hardened skeptics who resisted him, who walked away from his forums, lectures, prayer sessions, rallies, and group meditations, shaking their heads and spouting the same invectives and rejectives they without fail carried with them wherever they went, whatever the occasion.

But most people who experienced Apocalypso came away convinced, infected by his passion and hope-filled vision of personal and social perfection. Pumped up by the collective enthusiasm of the crowd at the events, they made firm if somewhat ephemeral commitments to promote and spread his world view and spiritual teachings.

Tonight's crowd was no exception. The rally which consisted of four minutes of inspiration and four hours of celebration would carry on into the night.

Billy had a splitting headache, the source of which could have been any number of things. High on the list of possibilities was a new bag of dope he had just scored, which he suspected again was laced with defoliants compliments of the DEA's helicopters over Hawaii and northern California. The sweat and noise of the crowd at the rally contributed their share to his misery.

They left early. No one seemed to notice.
"So, Candy. What did you think? Are we still friends?"
"Are you rich?"
"Do I look rich?"
"No. But it's the only hope for our continuing friendship. And the price is way up there."
"So, you weren't impressed."

"I'm impressed by results. I hope the guy can get the lard-asses moving. But frankly I have my doubts."

"What do you mean? I didn't see any lard-asses there tonight. I thought it was a tasteful display of body-conscious underground chic."

"Do you write for Fashion Week? You should."

"I try to see the good in everyone."

"Right. I was referring to the bulk of Americans."

"Clever pun, girly."

Candy burst out laughing. She laughed all the way to the subway station.

Then she became very quiet.

On the train, she turned to Billy. She looked tormented. Uncharacteristically afraid.

"I think I'm in love."

"Anybody I know."

"I don't think so."

"Oh . . . I see."

She closed the gap between them, put her nearest arm inside his, laid her other arm across his stomach and pulled herself as close to him as she could. She appeared anxious, expectant. A nun with wire-rim spectacles seated across from them peered over a Midnight Tattler she was reading, and gave them a fleeting look of disapproval.

Over the noise of the subway car, Billy didn't hear what Candy then softly said.

"Billy, it's you."

# A Drying Day

*Vivienne McCulloch*

It's Monday. I strip the bed. Off with the white linen embellished with faux-suede dots in shades of blue. On with my favourite; thick, crinkly antique cream cotton with raised embroidered lines. He says it reminds him of a Victorian christening dress. He doesn't like it. I think it is very modern.

The washing machine hums to a smooth finish. I take the basket out to the garden. I have a rotary washing line. When we moved here last year I was determined to have a decent washing line. I had to share a line-and-pulley one with upstairs in our last place. That caused a few awkward moments. Here, upstairs have their own garden and their own line. We have our own garden but there was no line when we moved in. I chose a big, sturdy four-section rotary and he concreted it into the middle of the little lawn. Nice and straight, too.

I start with the pillowcases. I peg them by their closed ends on the inner lines of the sections, two to each section. Two cream, for our foot pillows. Four blue, two for each head. Finally, two white ones with faux-suede dots in shades of blue, one for each head. I peg out a white bath towel and a blue hand towel each on two opposing sections. I am picking up the blue, fitted sheet to peg on the third section when I notice someone watching.

Through a wide gap in the panel fencing nailed to the garden wall my neighbour peers intently. She is perhaps a few years older than me. Her grey, flyaway hair is lifting in the light breeze, but her eyes are unmoving. I carry on pegging even though she knows I have seen her.

"Eight pillowcases?" she says.
"Oh, hello." I say.
"How comes you need eight?"
"Nice day, it should all dry lovely."

I smile a bit and spin the line to the last section. I pick up the white duvet cover with faux-suede dots in shades of blue. I have to pick it up in a certain way so I can peg it for optimum drying. First the top end. This gets pegged towards the back of the line embellished side down so the dots dry quicker. I should mention at this point that the duvet cover is inside out. This does stop the dots from fading in strong sunlight but the main reason is to make it easier to put on the duvet. I'll explain that another time.

"You know you've got that inside out?"
"Yes." I say.

It's not the first time I've seen her, of course. Last week she was looking at the bean frame I put up. I saw her from my dining room window. She went indoors and came back out a few minutes later with her husband. Then they both looked at it. He shook his head. He has the same unyielding eyes as his wife. I have the bottom end of the duvet cover folded concertina-like in my left hand. Now I unfold it, right to left, pegging the corners one at each end of the outermost line. Two pegs to a corner. Then I take up the inner unbuttoned side and peg it with one peg to the line behind. I use one more peg on the outer side securing it to the middle of the outer line.

"Never seen anyone do it like that before."

"Works for me."

I smile again and bend to put my candy-striped waterproof peg-bag in the empty plastic basket. When I stand up I see that her husband has appeared behind her. He takes a pipe from his mouth and waves it a bit.

"You won't dry all that today. Wasting your time. Going to thunder. A real downpour."

There is a dark cloud-bank very low on the horizon. The air is not that heavy yet. It won't come in until tea-time. By then my washing will be dried, picked in, aired, folded and put away. I don't iron linen

She turns to him. "Eight pillowcases!"

"Oh yes, why's that then?"

"Won't tell me."

He looks at me. His chin is jutting out a bit now. He stabs the air with the end of his pipe.

"Why won't you tell her?"

She has a triumphant look in her eyes. First time I've seen any expression in them.

"Excuse me?" I don't smile at him.

"Tell her why you got eight pillowcases." His face has gone a bit red now and his lower lip is sticking out.

I pretend to think about it. "No." I say.

"You got a cheek, so you have! You tell her now, or, or..." He is thrusting his shoulder past his wife and waving his pipe a lot.

I pick up my basket and walk smartly up my path. I can hear them arguing with each other as I shut the kitchen door behind me.

I make coffee, take two digestive biscuits from the airtight box, put them on a plate and go into the sitting room. My phone is on the low table, flashing. Four missed calls from my sister. As I put it down it rings again.

"Hiya."

"Where are you?"

"I'm home."

"I've been ringing you."

"I was pegging out the sheets."

"You could put your phone in your pocket. It is mobile."

I take a bite of digestive biscuit. "Good weekend?"

"Not bad. We booked our holiday. Vegas again, but this time we've got tickets for Celine. I'm so excited. Have you decided on yours yet? Or are you just going for your usual little trip to the Scillies?"

I sip my coffee. "You know she's having twins in November?"

"You're joking."

"Unless you're going very soon, don't be expecting to see her this year."

"Oh my God. I'll have to get this sorted. Ring you later."

"Bye."

I wash up my plate and mug and get out my polishing cloths. Before I start I dock the iPod and set it to play one Dead Weather and two White Stripes albums. Not too loud. By the time they have finished the flat is sparkling clean and it is lunchtime.

The Costcutter shop on the next street is very good but today it is out of tomatoes so I have to re-think tonight's dinner. No, I can make a Caesar salad to go with the salmon. That's alright then. He won't mind croutons for once. I pick up a newspaper and take it to the check-out. The woman looks at the front page as she passes it through the scanner.

"Four-one." She shakes her head. "Four-one – what was the matter with them?"

"I don't know."

"I said to you last week, I said they weren't looking themselves, remember?"

"I remember."

She takes my money. She's not wearing her England tee-shirt today.

"That bloody manager wants his arse kicked all the way back to Italy." It is my neighbour. He is behind me, waving his *Daily Mail*. His face is red again. There is a pause while he glares at me. It is very hot in the shop. I smile at them both, take my newspaper and leave.

Upstairs is in her garden. She has an assortment of clothing pegged neatly to her line-and- pulley. Just the one row today.

"I think it will dry alright today?" She looks a bit anxious.

"Should do." I look to the north-west. "It won't come in until tea-time."

She smiles, gently. I can hear my neighbour behind me, huffing down the road. I give upstairs a wave and go indoors.

I spend the afternoon at the dining table, sewing. I am making a wall hanging in silk and satin. It is an abstract design mostly in shades of blue. I put *La Mer* on quietly in the background, followed by *Fingal's Cave* and then some Satie to wind down. When *Gymnopedies* ends, I put my sewing away.

The neighbours are out in their garden again. I can't hear what they're saying, but the sounds are tense and heavy, blending with the hot air coming in through the open window as I prepare the salmon parcels for our dinner. I pick up the washing basket and go into the garden.

The cloud-bank is boiling up rapidly. It will be overhead soon. I fold the linen carefully as I take it off the line, stacking it neatly in the basket. Towels first, then the duvet cover, sheet, and finally the eight pillowcases. I tuck the basket under one arm and walk up my path. Now the temperature is dropping and I can hear thunder not far to the north-west. There is no sign of the neighbours.

I put away the linen. I won't start the salmon until I hear him close the gate. There is nothing more disappointing than overcooked salmon, especially if you have been looking forward to it all day. This gives me time to tidy a bookshelf. I have finished arranging his *Journal of Marine Science* by date and am starting on *Journal of Plankton Research* when I hear an ambulance siren. I go to my dining-room window. The ambulance pulls up next door.

The paramedics wheel him out, strapped in a sitting position. The left side of his face has fallen like a hillside after heavy rain. His body seems a lot smaller under the layers of red blanket. Behind them, coat and bag in hand, his wife hurries to lock their front door. She looks very tired now. There is a red, square-shaped welt swelling on her right cheek.

A long rumble of thunder rolls overhead. The first fat drops of rain hit the window. I hear the front gate squeal. Time to put the salmon in.

# Body Parts

*Kathleen Doherty*

I was heading to school with my daughter. I drive, she talks.

"My life is over."

"You're kidding, right? How did you come to this?" I ask her. I'm approaching the Greenwood Village speed trap and looking for 'donut cop' on his bike, wearing his Arapahoe County blue shirt stretched to the max.

"Mom, you drive like an old lady, no cop will ever ticket you."

"Fine. Why are you old?" Oops. "I mean, why is your life over?"

"Thanks for that. You think so too. Anyhow, I'm getting married and then after that what is there – really?"

"There's finishing school, there's hopefully a better

job, and travel if you two don't want kids. Making a life for yourself."

"So what does that look like? I'm not thinking it's so great." I do my best not to sigh, but I can't pull a quick smart Mom answer out of my bag of tricks.

"Seriously, what is there? We exist, right? We get married, we work, we pay bills, we buy stuff, we travel and pay bills. What is there?"

Mothers pick their battles. This is not one I want to engage in. My stomach lurches and I think, "Wow, even my stomach is upset at her line of thought." That or the Havarti cheese at lunch. I stay quiet while she continues her monologue. Was I such a fatalist at twenty-five? I manoeuvre the car into the school garage, park and get out. I feel worse - how in the world can this one-sided argument make me physically sick? I lay my head on my arm against the side of the car.

"What is wrong?" my daughter demands, grabbing her plaid book bag and slamming the car door closed.

"I'm trying not to throw up." I mutter. She looks relieved and pushes her sunglasses back on her head.

"Oh. Wow, I thought you were mad, you got so quiet." I have a presentation to give during the second class. I have to feel better; these are our last classes before break.

"Let's go grab a 7-up. Maybe that will help me. I think it's gas."

"Well, can we go to the bathroom first? Long commute, lot's of coffee."

"Sure. Maybe that will help." It doesn't. I go to wash my hands and she comes out and looks at me, frowning.

"You don't look so good, Mom. Why don't you hang out in the car until the second class and rest?"

"No, I came all the way down here and I already parked. I can do this." We walked towards the student union building and into the mini-mart where the line is wrapped out the door. I grabbed a Sprite and looked at the clock – we're going to be late. The girl ahead of me tried to use her credit card for a package of gum – the credit card machine was down. She began fumbling through her purse, pulling out random and various coins, talking on her cell phone the entire time.

"I know; that's what I'm saying. I mean, like what is he thinking not even calling me. Hello – I have a cell phone. I'm talking to you aren't I? It's just so – so bad – and then when he does call and I don't like answer – mmmm- hang on, hang on, someone's calling – Hello? Oh, hi honey! Oh I've been waiting for you to call – but listen, hon, can I, can you call me back in a few – yeah, that would be great, mm-hmm – yeah, love you honey, bye –yeah, that was him, whatever...oh wait a sec, I need to find one more dime..."

Sweat started down my back as I stood, waiting. I watched the clock, the girl, the cashier, sensed the line getting longer behind me every minute. My daughter began to pull cash out for the soda, but I had it ready before Cell Girl cleared the door. The cashier looked at me in relief at seeing someone with Cash In Fist.

We went back to my car again to retrieve my projector, laptop, books – none of which I was looking forward to carrying between two buildings and an intersection. We managed to beat the professor to the classroom and I went back to the bathroom again – it had to be gas. No luck. I trudged back to the classroom and tried to quietly open the soda and get situated with pen, notebook.

The professor walked in and launched into his lecture. I stared at the board ahead of me, focusing on the metal strip holding the chalk to help me ignore the pain running across the top of my rib cage – or at least where I believed my rib cage to be last located. My daughter sat next to me and hissed over to me.

"Get out of here!"

"No, I have a presentation next class!"

"You look awful."

"Too bad."

"You're pissing me off!"

The professor glanced at us and we sat back up – or tried to. I couldn't get comfortable. I decided that maybe I had to leave, after all. My daughter had a point. Was I really going to be able to pull off a presentation if I was this sick? And I didn't seem to be getting better. I tried one sip of Sprite – yuck. I stared hard at my notebook, not able to hear a word of the lecture. Okay, then, I can't make it – because I have to get out of here right now.

I don't remember or sense the noise of my pop bottle hitting the floor. All I knew was that I had to leave - ASAP. I bent down, retrieved the projector and backpack with the laptop. I clutched my pop bottle and placed it on the desk, then looked at my daughter and tried to smile and joke.

"Don't open that thing, hear? Can you get my books?" She nodded. The professor looked at me, no doubt amazed that I was deciding to interrupt his lecture – and trying to make light of it.

"Are you okay?" he asked. I scooped up my coat and ducked around him.

"Not really." I said. I headed out, not looking back. This abrupt exit would cost me, but I was in too much pain to really care. It was the worst case of gas ever and I had had some horrific cases of gas in my life. I got to the car and crawled in, driving home – in the middle of rush hour traffic.

I got to a lane and a speed at which I figured I could safely call my daughter's fiancé, Mannox. I explained the situation and that he would need to drive to the campus and pick her up.

"Well, how do I get there? I mean, can you give me directions?" he asked. I squeezed my eyes tight while stopped and tried to breathe out, expelling all the air. What the hell did they say in Lamaze classes? Pant like a dog? I can't pant; the pain is not letting up.

"Uhhh, look, just get on the interstate, get off at Colfax, turn right at Seventh. It's easy, there won't be any traffic."

"What about cross streets? Can you give me those?" The pain began to shoot across my stomach again; I gritted my teeth.

"Uhhh, no, look, I need to hang up and drive. Call her cell; she can talk you in, Okay?"

"Sure, no problem. Feel better." I would like to - I began counting to see if that would help. Maybe it's a tubal pregnancy? No, it can't be; I haven't been sexually active in years, decades. Maybe you can get that without having sex. Great. I pulled off at my exit and kept driving. I kept breathing whatever way made me feel more comfortable – which is a way of saying, not in shrieking pain.

I pulled the car into the garage, dragged myself out of it and grabbed a can of sparkling water. Somehow I got into the house. Where was the lemon juice? It was my standby cure for gas and usually would kick it right out of me within mere minutes. I changed into my nightgown and swallowed as much of my miracle concoction as fast as I could. Then I tried to lie down in my bed, even granting myself a few moans - which was ridiculous since I was home alone no one could even hear me. However, lying down was not something my body was going to let me do; the pain continued. I got up, tore through my bathroom for some indigestion pills and swallowed them with more of my concoction. Then I wrapped myself up in a blanket and tried to sleep. Not a chance. My stomach was having none of it.

Should I go to the hospital?

It's only gas – horrid gas, granted, but gas. And it's gas that doesn't seem to want to leave via any normal routes, by any type of encouragement.

Hmmm.

What if the people at the hospital say it's just gas, and send me home? I'm going to have to pay a big co-pay for that. Hmmm. I twisted around to get some relief, gave up, pulled at my headboard to get myself into a sitting position and got up.

I dialled my next door neighbor, The General. She has earned that title by stepping in and taking charge of every possible wayward urchin in our neighborhood, not to mention enforcing, for everyone's own good, various rules of the HOA we live under.

"Hello?"

"General, I need you to do something for me. Without freaking out. Okay?"

"What is it?"

"I need a ride to Main street Adventist."

"What's that?"

"It's a hospital, you moron. You work in this town and you don't even know the name of your own hospital?"

"It sounded like a church. Okay, fine. What's

wrong?"

"I have gas."

"What?"

"I think it's gas. I don't know. It's not going away."

"Okay. We'll be over in a few." I bent over and tried to do whatever I could to get rid of this gas. Nothing. At this rate, I was going to explode like a runaway Macy's balloon. I got back upstairs, pulled my clothes back on, grabbed my wallet (they will want money, no doubt), and edged downstairs out the door. The General's husband had the car backed up on the driveway. I slid in the front, ignoring the seat belt, and closed the door.

"What's wrong? What is it? How do you feel? Can you describe it?" I closed my eyes. I'd forgotten to tell her not to give me the inquisition ordeal.

"I don't know. I think it's gas. They had better not send me home without giving me something because this sucks. It's worse than labor."

"It's your gall bladder. Mmm-hmm. That's right. Gall bladder." I turned my head back at her.

"You don't know that."

"My sister's a nurse, she knows. It's a gall bladder, betcha, mmmhmmm. Honey, step on it. Watch you don't speed."

I sighed. "Whatever."

The General's husband did make excellent time and turned into the lane where the hospital was.

"Uhhh, I don't know where I need to go here..." he began. Not to worry, the General pointed out the obvious.

"Well, honey, it's right there, for heaven's sake, just point to it, can't you see she's in pain? " He made a turn too quick in one of the new roundabouts that took us away from the hospital. I squeezed my eyes shut against the pain and the barrage that was about to happen.

"Ahhh *shit!*"

"Well honey, you can see that this is not the way...now why..." I groaned.

"Gen, for the love of God, shut the hell up!" I looked sideways at her husband, who had a small grin forming on his face. "Don't get too excited, there. I'm in pain, I'm not taking sides."

"Ohhhh, but I am sooo enjoying the moment." We got to the main entrance. I got out rather than ask to go to the ER; moving seemed better for some reason. The General hopped out with me and marched to the doors. Since she has a good six inches on me in height and didn't have any gas pain, she was moving at a good clip. I stumbled along behind her resembling Quasimodo with asthma. She would turn and scowl and wave her frantic arms at me to hurry, hurry. I would continue my stumbling, lurching gait, but I held back from swinging my arms and saying, "Yes, Master."

The ER was empty aside from one kid with a paper cut that was ahead of me. The clerk looked at me without any possible expression that I could note.

"What seems to be the problem?" I wanted to scream but it was probably not her fault that I had this gas from that Havarti cheese. Anyhow, it didn't matter – the General stepped in.

"She's in a lot of pain. In her abdomen. She says it's gas. However, I think it's gall bladder."

I growled at her, but she ignored me.

"What is your pain level from one to ten?"

"I'm at about twenty." I gasped.

"No, between one and ten."

"Fine. Ten."

"I need your insurance card. Here's some paperwork. Have you visited us before?" Why yes, I was here last during your semi-annual white sale.

"Yes, I'm a frequent flyer." Still no expression. She scanned her screen. "Oh, yes you have. Vertigo, how interesting. Oh and migraines."

"I'm still getting those, by the way." She turned away. I walked over to the chairs and started writing on the forms, thinking about *Grey's Anatomy*. How come they never show this part of the process? The General hovered over me; I looked up at her and rolled my eyes. "Sit. Stay. Good General." I raced through the paperwork (because I have already *been here before and you have this information*). I managed to walk over and hand her the clipboard.

"Okay, thanks. There's one ahead of you." Who takes their kid to the ER for a paper cut? Maybe he's a hemophiliac, though. I'd better not raise a fuss. He and his parents are called a few minutes later. I get called about fifteen minutes later – I think – I'm not sure because I'm starting to lose sense of time. The General comes with – ordering her husband to stay who isn't too interested in coming anyhow. We go into triage – like *MASH*. I sit, or I try but by now I am really hurting and I am digging my nails into the armrests. Not an easy thing to do, since they're wood and not padded. All the same, I'm leaving my mark.

"Okay, I need to get some vitals from you and some information." This is where the General comes in very handy.

"You have her information. She's been here before, she has yet again filled out the same information and her name and address have not changed since she got here. So how about just getting her vitals since she is in some pretty horrendous pain, okay?" He glares at her, but pulls out his triage kit. I am gripping the armrests with all my force from the pain.

"Stop that right now!" he barks. "I need to get your blood pressure." I see The General's hand come up, and I signal, *no*. We get done and he snaps a couple bracelets on me, thereby admitting me further into the hospital, or at least away from him. We go to yet another room, but at this point, they are setting up an IV. This may not be gas.

One of the male nurses comes in and hands me a gown. "Hop on into bed, honey, I don't think you'll be going anywhere for a while." He isn't joking; we end up waiting for orders to come through, by which time The General is pacing and ready to start taking on the entire hospital.

An intern shows up, gets an IV going, and another male nurse shows up – Scott, who could forget the name of the person who brings you drugs, right? – Who shot something in the IV to start me out on and had to keep upping it. I didn't care, he took the pain away, he was my savior – I may have proposed to him at some point.

A lab tech came in and mentioned that my white count was pretty elevated so they wanted to keep me. They also wanted me to get an ultrasound, blah, blah, blah, whatever it is they say on *Grey's Anatomy*. Scott had to follow my bed down the hall to the ultrasound at a trot with the meds to keep me out of pain. The tech there took one look and snapped at me, "We're done here. How did you miss this?" I looked at him like he was the professor I walked out on earlier.

"Miss what?"

"This. Here. Your gall bladder is packed full of gallstones. How did you not know that?"

Perhaps because my home ultrasound machine was repossessed?

"I uh, I don't, uh, know."

"You mean to tell me tonight is the very first time you have had any kind of pain?" He folded his arms and stared at me.

"Well, I'm not in the medical field. I thought it was gas." Scott wheeled me back to the holding room.

"Wow, so I flunked his test." I muttered. Scott laughed. He informed The General and her husband that it was my gall bladder and all indications were that it was going to have to come out. I needed to wait for a room – and a surgeon – in whatever order that should come.

The General could not have been happier; she glowed with satisfaction, pausing only to remind me of how she just knew, just knew what it was. There was no silencing her. She called my daughter and her fiancé, waited for them to show up and then left me for them to take over the watch.

The surgeon arrived eventually. Of course he was handsome – why not? *Grey's Anatomy*, right? "Hi there, I hear you're not feeling so good. I think your gall bladder needs to come out, which will make you feel a lot better very shortly." At this point, knowing it's not gas, and rolling between valleys of pain and some brainless drug-induced state, I'm quite agreeable to anything except that I realize my hair has a one inch skunk line of gray and I may have not shaved my legs. I roll toward my daughter.

"Oh God, he's hot. And I didn't shave my legs, "I whisper. At least I think – or hope – I whispered. She looked at me with one of her looks she reserves for special morons that pester her at her coffee shop.

"I think he'll take care of that."

I smile at him."Okay, take whatever. Just get rid of this pain." He's got the bedside manner down to an art form, takes my hand in his (his hands are really warm) and smiles. Nice eyes. Brown. I like brown eyes. I have brown eyes. Maybe we're related. Wait. Wedding ring – *stop*.

"So I'm going to try and do this by laparoscopy. Do you know what that is?" I nod. "If I can't, we'll need to open you up, but let's try laparoscopy first which is a few small incisions. I usually perform this on an outpatient basis. It's minimally invasive. I promise you that once we get that out you will feel a whole lot better. I have a few scheduled ones ahead of you but I'm going to work you in later in the day, alright? In the meantime, we'll keep you as comfortable as we can."

I don't bother saying that if there's a knife handy I can take it out right now and save everyone some time, as long as I can get some relief.

"Hey, wait. Can I watch?" My daughter has suddenly come to life from the other side of the bed. He looks at her.

"What?"

"Can I watch the operation? I think it would be interesting." He looks down at me and then over to her.

"This is your mother, right?"

"Well, yes, of course. She won't mind."

"This uh, isn't a training hospital."

"Okay. Can I get the gall bladder then?"

"What? Why?"

"I've never seen one..."

"No, we need to have that; you can't just take it..."

"It belongs to my mom, not you. I should get to keep it." I'm suddenly feeling like a side of beef at a butcher shop.

"What in the world are you going to do with it? Wait – what, no, you cannot have it."

"Okay, how about a couple gallstones?" Maybe I'm at a Christie's auction, not a butcher shop. He sighs.

"I'll see. I suppose you'd like a kidney too." I snap my head toward him.

"Wait, I need mine don't I?"

"It won't be yours. Let me see what I can do." He makes his exit.

My daughter folds her arms. "I don't see why I can't at least watch. I'll scrub up and everything."

"No, you'll be the one that drops the damn Junior Mint in me," I say, referring to a *Seinfeld* episode. Sometime later I made it to surgery, though the entire ordeal is one long drug trip. I remember trying to work a deal with one of the nurses for their scrub hat. Since I came home without one, I am assuming that the deal fell through.

I found myself back in my room with the migraine from hell and really not feeling well, though the nurse on duty was pleased that the laparoscopy was a success. I begged for drugs and hours later I got them and perked right up. My daughter and the fiancé came in.

"Well you look much better than you did yesterday", said my daughter's fiancé.

"Did you get any sleep?" my daughter asked. "You still look tired." Behind her green eyes I could see the fear slowly ebbing away. Smart ass comments aside, I'm the last parent standing. She would prefer to keep me that way for awhile.

"No, I have to go home to sleep. When do I get out of here?'

"I don't know. We missed the doctor; we went out

to eat while you were in surgery and he left before we got back because he had four more waiting. The guy's a machine."

"I don't think they will keep me too long because he said this is usually done on an outpatient gig. But I feel so much better. I had a migraine that sucked. And these nurses are all trying to fix me up with a date, so I need to get out of here." Mannox laughed.

"I didn't get the damn gallstones! I missed him because we went to eat!" my daughter said, exasperated. "He said he came out, we weren't there, so I missed my chance."

"That or it's an excuse. Maybe it's against some stupid law." I said. "Well, they belong to you. You should have a say so in who gets them."

She switched topics. "If you get released, who can take you home?"

"I guess The General. Do you two have plans?"

"We got invited to a party. Do you mind? It's my birthday weekend so I was going to go." Suddenly there may be a something to life, she had decided. Beyond twenty-five, life may not all end after some ridiculous ceremony next year.

"Well, let me call The General. I would prefer not to have to climb into Mannox's pick-up truck. I can take a cab, I guess." My daughter rolled her eyes.

"Oh let me pack my bags – Mom's sending me on another guilt trip." Now it was my turn to roll my eyes.

"Oh shush, I don't even know when I'm getting out."

"Well, you should go home today. Now. This place is not helping you."

"Wouldn't you rather I stayed here one more night so you know someone is watching me?"

"Not really. I think The General does a better job."

"Well, let me see what they say, I will do my best to get sprung and if I run into an issue I'll call you but assume I have it under control and I'm going home otherwise, okay? And thank you."

"For what?"

"Pfft! For sitting up with me and dealing with me, you putz."

I have since recovered, though at the time, my co-workers have decided that there may be a market for a t-shirt with 'I Thought It Was Gas.' One manager sent out an e-mail warning people that he saw a gall bladder bouncing down the hall and was wondering if it was mine. The final comment was the one guy made the comment that while all gave some, I definitely gave all.

The professor at school was not impressed with my exit or my excuse. I pointed out that I did try to minimize the impact on his lecture. Nonetheless, I ended up with a B, not an A. Whether body part drama had something to do with that was never determined.

I was told I didn't need it – I am surviving without it. So what really is a gall bladder?

# Stella's Starwish

*Erica Verrillo*

I'd been working at Shady Grove almost a year the morning Clarence moved in. It wasn't a day I would have remembered otherwise, since it started fairly typically with Mama red-eyed on the sofa and Hector passed out on the kitchen floor. Nothing new on the home front. It was wall-to-wall traffic all the way up I-10, as usual. My AC was on the fritz, so the commute was literally hell on wheels, and the only thing my radio was picking up was ET trying to make first contact. Beam me up, I thought. No such luck.

After I'd changed into my uniform, Mrs. Jackson took me over to meet the new inmate.

"Mr. Savage," said Mrs. Jackson. "This is Stella. She'll be cleaning your room." Mr. Savage bobbed his head at me. They were all polite when they first arrived. Once he'd gotten used to the place he'd be pinching my butt and hissing dirty jokes in my ear along with the rest of them.

"I'm so glad you've decided to join us, Mr. Savage," I recited. "If you need anything, please don't hesitate to call. We pride ourselves on prompt and courteous service."

Mrs. Jackson beamed at me. It had taken her hours of hard work to get The Speech crammed down my throat. The fact that the janitorial staff was never needed for "prompt and courteous service" meant nothing to her. Neither did the *Emancipation Proclamation* or the *Bill of Rights*.

"You can call me Clarence," he said. I expected that. While Mrs. Jackson always insisted that we address everyone by their family names so as to "preserve an atmosphere of propriety," nobody else followed her example, especially not towards the staff. I was always plain old Stella right from the get go.

That morning I went about my normal routine. Cleaning up the public rooms came first, since most of the old folks slept in. I guess there isn't much point to getting up early when all you're doing is dying. I always started with the chapel. I enjoyed the quiet. There wasn't much of that at home. Best of all it was cool. Hector was too cheap to put in central air, so my room was an oven in the summer even with the window unit, which hardly worked anyway. I liked to sit in the front pew for a few moments before I got on with my rounds, just to gather my thoughts. After the chapel was clean, I moved on to the public bathrooms, the dining room, the rec room, and the TV room. By then most of the old folks were tottering about, so I could start on their bedrooms. When I got to Mr. Savage's room I banged on his door and waited. On my very first day of work at Shady Grove, Mrs. Jackson told me to always knock real hard and call out their names. She said we needed to respect the 'members' personal space.' I was much more concerned with my own. Some of the men had an uncanny way of popping up stark naked when you came in to clean. I hoped Mr. Savage wasn't going to be one of those.

"Mr. Savage!" I hollered. I began counting to thirty before I turned the key. That would give him plenty of time to come to the door if he was still in there. I was pretty sure he wouldn't be, since Mrs. Jackson liked to take her new 'members' for a tour of Shady Grove the day after they arrived. She liked to tell them all about the 'estate' and how it had been in her family for generations and all that la-de-dah. So it just about knocked my socks off when the door opened smack in my face. I hadn't even made it to five.

"I can hear just fine," he said. He was wearing pressed slacks and a green plaid shirt buttoned all the way to the top.

"I'm sorry," I apologized. "Some of the members..."

"I understand," he said. "You can come in."

I peeked into his room. It was neat as a pin.

"I'll only be a minute," I said. Maybe less. His room was already so clean I probably wouldn't have to do much more than mop. I waited a moment for Clarence to go away, but he just stood there holding the door open. As I angled past him I noticed that he didn't smell like a shut-in. Old people, when they've been housebound for a while, start to smell musty. Clarence smelled like a man who worked with his hands. Clean and sharp. He watched me as I mopped the linoleum, which made me nervous.

"Y'all are gonna love it here. Everybody's real friendly, and nice. And when the weather cools off all y'all can take a walk in the old pecan grove." I tend to rattle on when I get nervous. "Y'all can even send some pecans home to your loved ones next Christmas. Everybody does." I took a breath. Clarence was looking at me funny. I noticed that his eyes were a clear gray.

"All y'all?" he said. His face was round and pleasant when he smiled, but my feathers had been ruffled.

"You aren't from around here, are you?" I said, real slow.

His face got serious again. "No," he said. "I'm from Maine."

I'd already taken him for a Yankee. His skin was too smooth for a Texan, even a transplanted one. Old Texans don't have wrinkles, they have ruts. Still, my jaw dropped. Maine was on the other side of the world. I couldn't imagine a farther place.

"How on earth did you get down here?" The question just fell out of my mouth. Then I realized I'd forgotten my manners, so I had to apologize again.

"No, no," he said. "That's a good question. We Yankees find Texas fascinating. It's the lure of the Old West."

Having lived in Texas my whole life, I didn't see anything luring about the West, old or new. But I had a Texan's pride in my state, which is to say, knee-jerk. The only real requirement for graduation in Texas is to remember the Alamo, which we did every spring, regardless of the fact that most of my classmates would likely have been fighting on the other side.

"See y'all tomorrow," I said. His smell stayed with me all day. Like Christmas.

By the time I got home, Mama and Hector had made up and were watching TV on one of the velveteen couches. Mama has three of them. With Mama, everything is either too many or too much. Hector had one arm draped around her and the other wrapped around a six-pack. The two of them were drunk as two skunks courting in Kentucky.

"Yo, mamacita," said Hector.

I hate it when he calls me that. In spite of appearances, and a lot of effort on his part, Hector doesn't have a drop of Spanish blood in him. Mama, on the other hand, is a direct descendent of Don Quixote.

Hector tried to grab my butt when I walked by, but I was ready for him. My purse has a five-pound mini barbell in it. Mama never shifted her fake eyelashes from the screen.

"That's disgusting!" she said. Some idiot was chowing down on a plate of worms. She took a swig of beer.

"There's spaghetti," she said.

Somehow, I managed to get back to my room without having to hit Hector again. The house was a classic Texas "shotgun" with one long central hall going from front to back. It was a simple design, but whoever built it hadn't been sober long enough to read a blueprint. There wasn't a ninety-degree angle in the place, and all the doors opened the wrong way; out instead of in. If you weren't careful, you could brain someone, not that anybody who lived on this side of the tracks had any.

I switched on the window unit, but all it did was bitch and moan. Just like an eighth-grade boyfriend, all jaw and no action. I appreciated the racket. It blocked out the noises Hector and Mama would be making later on.

That night I dreamed about the Titanic again. I especially like the part where it goes down.

I liked Clarence. He never asked questions like: didn't I have a boyfriend, and how many boyfriends had I had, and he never, ever treated me like a servant. At first I couldn't resist boasting. I'd heard Texas described a lot of ways, but never, to my knowledge, had anybody called it "fascinating." As far as I was concerned, Texas was nothing more than a giant griddle, flat as a pancake and hotter than Hades. Of course, I never let on. The fact that he thought it was interesting made me feel good¾like I was special too, somehow. And Clarence was a good listener. When he sat down and cocked an ear at me, it made me stand up tall. In fact, I got so high and mighty it took a couple of weeks for me to realize I didn't know a thing about him, which was not the normal run of events. Usually, after two or three days I could recite an inmate's life story by heart.

"What's Maine like?" I asked.

"The interior is mostly woods," he said. "But I grew up on the coast. In my younger days, I was a lobsterman," he added. "Later on, I built boats."

I should have guessed. That clean, sharp smell was sawdust. I could see him in a workshop, sawing something. Although, I have to say, I couldn't imagine Clarence pulling those big ugly red things out of the water. With those evil-looking claws grabbing at you, how in god's creation did you get the hook out? You probably had to bash 'em upside the head with a sledgehammer, which I couldn't see neat-and-tidy

Clarence doing. Anyway, Clarence didn't smell like the fishing type. Fishermen drank.

"I've never seen the ocean," I said.

This time it was his turn to look surprised.

"Well," he said. "It's big."

I knew what he was talking about. Texas is big.

"I know all about big," I told him. "I could drive all day and never even make it out of this county."

Clarence pulled on his chin and thought about that for a while. I could tell I'd impressed him.

"Ayuh," he said. "I had a car like that once."

Well, I just about popped my panties laughing.

"That's a very old joke," he said, shaking his head. "You must have heard it before."

I hadn't, but I didn't want to be shown up by quiet Clarence. Besides, I really had seen big bodies of water. My entire 10th grade class had taken a field trip to the capital, and on the way back we'd stopped for a picnic on Lake Travis. I told him about it.

"The ocean is a lot bigger," he said.

"Well, that may be," I admitted. "But I'll bet you dimes to dollars you couldn't swim across Lake Travis."

Now it was his turn to laugh, though I didn't know why.

"You won that bet," he said. "I couldn't swim across a bathtub."

I looked at him sceptically. I was beginning to get the suspicion that he had been pulling my leg all along. "You said you caught lobsters."

"I did," he said. "Lobstermen can't swim. The water off the coast of Maine is so cold, if you fell overboard you'd be dead in ten minutes."

He swirled his tea, making the ice cubes clink against the sides of the glass. "It's like ice," he said.

"That sounds real good," I told him. "I'd like that."

It was May, and the heat was just revving up. You couldn't fry an egg on the sidewalk yet, but you could probably poach one. Every morning I would arrive at work just itching to get Clarence into a conversation about that big old ice bath. I swear it made me feel cooler just to hear him talk about it. I'd lean up against the wall for a few minutes after I'd mopped, there never was anything else to do in Clarence's room, and I swear I could feel that cool sea breeze blowing right over me. He had a way of telling stories that would make me fall down laughing, though I could never remember how he did it afterwards. He would just sit in his chair, pulling his chin. Maybe it was because he'd made me laugh so much that I forgot my manners one day.

"How come you don't have any pictures on your dresser?" I asked him. Everybody else at Shady Grove had scads of family photos propped up on just about every surface. That's why it never took me any time to clean up Clarence's room. There was nothing to dust.

Clarence didn't answer me. So I just stood there like a moron until it dawned on me that I was way out of line. Stupid me. I'd forgotten Rule Number One: Staff is not permitted to make personal inquiries of Members.

"I'm sorry," I said. "I shouldn't have asked."

Clarence still didn't say anything. He looked out the window to where the crape myrtles were blooming. Crape myrtles are perfect for this climate. They bloom all summer long and don't mind the heat. I imagine that's why Mrs. Jackson's illustrious ancestors had planted them everywhere. On second thought, it was the gardeners who had planted them. My illustrious ancestors.

I was almost through the door when Clarence finally said something.

"My wife died a year ago last March," he said. "We didn't have any children."

Now, I felt terrible. "Oh, I am sorry," I said again. This time I meant it. Clarence looked so forlorn. All of a sudden I wanted to go over and hug him. Instead, I stood in the doorway like a fool, holding a mop and a bucket in my hands. Clarence shook his head and sighed.

"She was from Texas," he said.

I stood there for a bit, trying to think of something to say that would cheer him up. "Did she say all ya'll?" I asked. "Like me?"

Clarence looked me right in the eye. "Just like you."

Hector and Mama were going at it full blast when I got home. She was calling him an hijo de puta, which is the only thing she can say in Spanish, and he was yelling about somebody named Frank. I heard some thumps and crying. But it was a hundred and one degrees and after spending an hour getting honked at by suits yakking on their cell phones in Audis that had frickin' frost on the windows, I was in no mood to call the police. So I went to my room and turned on the AC as loud as it would go. I also turned on the radio for good measure. Then I stretched out on the bed, praying for world peace, for a sea of ice, for anything but this. I lay there for a while with my ears cocked, just in case things got really nasty. Then, in spite of the heat, Willie Nelson, and the sound of dishes flying around the kitchen, I fell asleep.

What woke me up was the quiet. The whole world was dead. I looked over at my clock and saw nothing. Outage. In the summer, with all of Texas trying to reinvent Alaska, the power frequently goes out. I got up and went to the window. There were lights on in some of the houses. Maybe it was just a blown fuse. I threw on a robe, since I wasn't wearing much, and tried to remember where the fuse box was. Or did we have switches?

My door wouldn't open.

I shoved and pushed and kicked, but it wouldn't budge. Something heavy was blocking it. Finally I started yelling, but nobody heard me; Mama and Hector were probably out cold. Eventually, my brains woke up. I went back to the window and pushed out the AC unit. Even though it didn't work, the thing still weighed a ton, just like Hector. Then I climbed out the window and hopped onto the lawn.

When I came around to the front of the house, I saw the door hanging open. Hector's car was gone, so he must have stormed off after tonight's fight, leaving the front door wide open. Total idiot, I thought. Don't y'all come back now.

The house was pitch black, but I knew it well enough to find what I needed. Neither Mama nor Hector had gotten around to opening any of the drawers in the kitchen, except, of course, for the one that had the bottle opener in it, so the flashlight was still where I'd put it when we moved in last year.

The kitchen was a wreck. But, that was to be expected. I hadn't gone in there for a few days, so there'd been plenty of time for TV dinner trays and dirty dishes to pile up. The cans were having a pow-wow on the floor with some broken plates and there was a bunch of empty bottles on the table. It looked like Hector and Mama had graduated to the hard stuff last night. Or maybe it had been that way all week. I hadn't been keeping track.

I walked out of the kitchen and headed down the hallway to the back of the house. There was something heaped in front of my door.

"Mama," I said. I shook her as hard as I could. When I tried to lift her, Mama's head snapped back like a broken doll.

I called 911.

When the ambulance arrived, I still hadn't been able to wake her. I hadn't even thought about the fuses, so I had to lead the medics through the house with my flashlight. I was glad they couldn't see most of it. But what they couldn't see they could smell. They took Mama straight to the detox unit of the hospital.

The doctor who finally came out to see me looked harried. It was four am.

"She'll need to stay here for a couple of weeks," he said, glancing at her chart. "Are you a relative?"

I said yes.

"Good," he said. "You'll have to sign some papers."

"Will she be all right?" I asked.

The doctor finally took a good look at me. "You aren't a minor, are you?"

"No," I said. "I turned eighteen last August." And if we'd been in China, that would have been god's honest truth.

"Good," said the doctor. "Go to the main desk. They'll have the papers ready."

He hadn't answered my question. After I signed the papers, the nurse told me that I should probably take a couple weeks off work. It might help Mama to have someone there for support. I asked her if Mama was going to be all right.

"That depends," she said.

There wasn't much I could say to that.

I called in sick and told Mrs. Jackson I needed some time off. She grumped about unreliable help, but didn't say I was fired. Thank god for small favors. Then I went back to bed, but I couldn't sleep. I felt like I needed to talk to somebody. I got into the car and drove to work, hoping that Mrs. Jackson wouldn't catch me on the premises. I'd have a hard time explaining my miraculous recovery from the plague.

Clarence looked so happy to see me, I felt like bawling.

"I thought you were sick," he said.

"No, my mother's not well." I said. "I'm going to have to take care of her for a couple of weeks."

Clarence waved me into his room and shut the door. He pulled up a chair for me, and then sat on the edge of his bed.

"Is there anything I can do?" His voice was so gentle, I didn't want to say anything. So, I just looked at him, sitting there in his green plaid shirt. Even first thing in the morning his eyes were clear and bright. He didn't look like the sort of person who had ever gotten falling down drunk, or tried to pinch his stepdaughter's butt, or carted his mother off to detox. He looked like... Maine.

"No," I said. "It's nothing I can't handle."

Clarence nodded and sighed. He knew I was in over my head. And what made me love him is that he didn't call me out on it. He respected my decision to keep my problems to myself. And I knew that whenever I wanted to talk, he'd be there. In the end that was all I really needed. Just knowing Clarence was there was enough.

We sat for a moment. Then Clarence got up and took something out of the top drawer of his dresser. He handed me a little box.

"Open it," he said. "I was going to save it for Christmas, but now seems to be a good time."

Inside the box was a rusty-looking thing with five points, like a star. The top of it was covered with tiny pimples. I didn't want to know what was on the bottom. It looked like something one of those weirdos on TV might eat if you offered him enough money.

"It's a starfish," he said.

It didn't look even remotely like a fish. But, then again, lobsters don't look like anything you'd want to put in your mouth either.

"Did you used to catch these things, too?" I asked.

"There's a note," he said. "Underneath."

I lifted up one corner of the starfish with tip of my fingernail and saw a small square of paper. A star for Stella, it said.

"Um," I mumbled. I wasn't good at getting gifts.

"Make a wish," he said. "It's a star."

"I don't have anything to wish for," I lied.

Clarence looked down at me. "Follow your dreams, Stella," he said. "While you still have them." He held out his hand for me to shake, an unusual gesture for him. He'd never touched me before. I said goodbye to him then.

"Y'all come back now," he said.

"Ayuh," I replied. "I'll send you a post card."

When I came back to work, I was excited about

seeing Clarence again. Hector had disappeared and Mama seemed to be doing much better without him. But, with her it was hard to get hopeful. Within a month or two she'd probably be slugging it out with her next Hector, or maybe the same one. In any case, I was glad for the peace and quiet, even if it was temporary. I'd brought Clarence a big Stetson, just for laughs. I was sure he wouldn't wear it.

It was early, so I put on my uniform and started on my rounds. The chapel was quiet, as always, but this morning it was filled with flowers. There was a casket on the dais.

Oh, no, I thought. Mrs. Perkins has finally died. Delia Perkins was in her nineties and as fragile as a china teacup. We all expected her to go any minute.

I walked over to the casket and peered inside. Lying within the pale satin interior was a man in a suit and tie. He looked familiar.

"Is that really you?" I said. Some idiot had put glasses on his face.

"Oh, Clarence," I whispered. "I bet you never wore glasses a day in your life."

At all once, I had to sit down. I must have sat in the front pew for an hour. That's about how long it takes me to make a decision. On my way out I gave Mrs. Jackson my notice. She didn't look at all surprised.

You can't count on young people nowadays," she said.

When the chapel was opened for the service, the glasses Mrs. Jackson had placed on Clarence were missing. On his head he wore a big, black Stetson hat. A note was tucked into the hatband: Gone fishin'.

On Christmas Eve, a post card arrived at Shady

Grove Estate addressed to a Mr. Clarence Savage. A box was kept in the main office for letters and cards such as these. In her spare time Mrs. Jackson would sit at her desk and inspect them for return addresses. She liked to write the letters of condolence herself. It gave Shady Grove that genteel touch for which it was famous. She held the card a moment in her hand, automatically looking at the picture. Inappropriately, given the time of year, it was a photograph of waves crashing violently against dark, jagged rocks.

"Not very Holiday-like," she murmured. Mrs. Jackson turned the card over. It was postmarked Southwest Harbor, Maine. There was no return address.

"Dear Clarence," she read. "You were right. It's bigger than Lake Travis. Wish y'all were here. Love, Stella."

# Galileo's Hood

*C B Heinemann*

The first time I performed on the street to avoid starvation was in Padua, Italy. I was travelling around Europe with three friends. Charlie and Terry came over with me, and Pete was a hard-drinking English guy we met at a music festival in France. Pete had a van and was afflicted by an extravagant case of verbal diarrhoea, talking non-stop through France, Germany, and Switzerland. Luckily, that affliction helped get us invited to crash at strangers' houses, to parties, and to play the occasional gig. We played in pedestrian zones by day and bars by night, making enough money to keep ourselves in wine and gas. Another busker told us that Italy was virgin territory for street performers, so while stuck in a week-long rainstorm in Switzerland watching our money disappear and our stomachs shrink, we studied our maps to plan an escape.

Padua was close to Venice, which we figured would be the juiciest busking peach in Italy. Charlie, who two weeks before our trip fell out of a third floor window and left the hospital just in time to make our flight, wanted to see the frescos by Giotto in the Scrovegni Chapel. Petrarch, Donatello, and Galileo also lived and worked in Padua, and we all know what happened to Galileo. Brimming with the vague sense of purpose we felt when journeying to a place we actually knew something about, we crossed over the Alps from the fastidious, logic-driven Northern World into the inscrutable, laid-back, tradition-soaked Southern World. The architecture ranged from magnificent to dreary, with graceful churches mingling with tacky post-war apartment buildings. Some villages we passed were so venerable that they seemed embedded in the crust of the earth, while our own century's technological litter of telephone cables, electric lights, and cars poked up like momentary pustules. The autostrade from Milan to Verona was a congested mess of factories, power lines, prefabricated shopping malls, dingy apartment buildings and gritty pollution, with the occasional glimpse of an olive grove or graceful villa. The road was clogged with trucks, and for long stretches, northern Italy was little more than an endless string of Clevelands.

By the time we got to Padua it was nearly midnight. European cities are like oysters—pearl-like antique centres surrounded by ugly shells of modernity. We spent an hour buzzing around the city like an insect looking for an opening, but every time we thought we found a street leading to the centre, a clever complex of one-way streets spat us back out again. At last we gave up and drove into the countryside to spend the night. The scent of unwashed males made the atmosphere in the van a bit too fruity, so we decided to sleep outside. We found a grassy spot by the creek in a small park, with several willows grouped together, where we couldn't see the lights from the surrounding buildings.

The next morning I opened one eye to see fog hanging over the park and an elderly woman walking her poodle trying to ignore us. The poodle, however, gave us a look that he might give a particularly ripe fire hydrant. We bundled up our damp bags and trudged back to the van while a group of children playing nearby stopped to shout at us and laugh.

Our tyres had been slashed and a side window smashed in. It was the work of an instant to ascertain that our communal bag of money was gone. The four of us were stuck thousands of miles from home, penniless in a country we had never before visited and knew nothing about. Standing in that little residential neighborhood staring at each other, we realized that we were literally starving on the streets of a foreign land. I felt a strange, existential sensation.

"Bloody bleedin' 'ell!" Pete shouted, swiping at the broken window and cutting his palm in the process. "And I was hoping for a bit of a vacation down here. We don't have any money, or any food. What the bleedin' 'ell do we do now?"

"Be glad we still have our instruments," I pointed out in an unappreciated attempt to see the bright side. "Otherwise we'd have to beg, or just lie down and die in the park."

Staggering under the weight of our backpacks and instruments, we picked our way through the swarming roads of Padua to the signs marking the boundaries of the pedestrian zone. We wandered through an area where the sidewalk was torn up, leaving dirt and concrete scattered in small piles, and then down a winding cobblestone alley. The buildings looked far older than any others we had yet seen in Europe. Most were pale ochre in color, with rust stains dripping like streaks of sweat down the sides. Clothes hung overhead from iron balconies and clotheslines strung over the narrow lanes. A sweet aroma of wet stone, cheese, and flowers filled the air. I was dizzy with hunger.

The walkway spilled onto the broad Piazza della Erbe, surrounded on all sides by beautiful Renaissance buildings. Each had its own arcaded walkway with elegant arching doorways. The ground floors of many buildings contained shops and cafes. Near the centre of the piazza stood dozens of carts piled with fresh produce, while behind them, ruddy-cheeked women chattered full volume in the rapid-fire cadence of Italian. In the centre of the square rose a magnificent renaissance structure with a food market on the ground floor. The upper floor looked like it might have housed an art museum. We later learned that it did.

The air was dense with the pungency of basil and the sugar of peaches. Water formed grid works of puddles around the worn cobblestones in the square, and hundreds of pigeons stalked with bobbing heads as they searched for bits of food-entire flocks taking off together while others swooped in to replace them. Old men stood reading newspapers or shouting at one another at close range. I eyed the pigeons, many of whom appeared to be quite plump and succulent.

We walked under a low archway that led to another piazza, Piazza della Fruitti, where dozens of white plastic tables sat near a row of cafes and restaurants. Exhausted, we decided to busk under the archway because everybody who wanted to go from one piazza to the other had to pass under it. A cramped pizza shop stood behind the nearest grape-laden cart, tucked away in the arcade, and I fixed my eyes on that shop.

Charlie started into a reel, *The Wise Maid*. He played the first part alone, and the singing tones of his flute danced through the echoes of the ancient stones. The second time through, Terry on fiddle, Pete on bodhran, and I, on bouzouki, plunged in, adding our own sounds to that place that saw and heard so much over the centuries.

A crowd formed immediately. The women of Padua stood tapping their feet and smiling as they held their bags of produce, the kids watching wide-eyed and clutching their mother's skirts. Several thousand lire notes appeared in the hat, and the crowd continued to grow. Even a pair of tiny old ladies, whose heads barely came up to Charlie's belt buckle, stopped to listen. After we played for about ten minutes to a generous crowd, we bolted into the cafe to shove something into our stomachs. We divided up the money with jittering fingers while waiting for the little pizzas to warm, and ended up with more than twelve thousand lire each.

"Not bad for a load of bloody derelicts who have to sleep in the park," Pete said as we relaxed a few minutes later at an outdoor table. "If it weren't for getting robbed on occasion, we could get rich around here in a few weeks time."

I opened my *Let's Go* guide to the section on Padua. "Look at this, right here. You won't believe this."

Charlie looked up from rolling a cigarette. "Some rare insect flattened between the pages?"

"There's a hotel nearby, right over there, where rooms are six thousand lire a night. That's four dollars."

The proprietor, Silvio, was a small, dark-haired man in his forties wearing a loosened tie, white shirt, and baggy black trousers. After a brief game of charades at his front desk, Silvio showed us to our room at the top of a narrow staircase. Before he left, he jingled the bunch of keys in his pocket and pointed to his watch. "Please, we close, meed-a-night, okay? Meed-a-night."

That afternoon we lounged in our hotel room popping fat grapes into our mouths. Outside, the old buildings glowed in the southern sun. Our beds stood in a line on one wall, with a crucifix over the door. Against the opposite wall leaned an ancient wooden dresser with a cracked marble top, and an aged porcelain sink slumped next to the door. The ceiling was high and the peeling walls were painted deep green decades earlier. To us it was a palace.

Our days in Padua drifted by under a scorching Italian sun. We rose early each morning to busk in the piazzas during the daily market, strolled a few blocks to the vast and ancient Basilica del Santo, played for the tourists, then retreated from the midday heat to shower, write letters, or doze. Eventually we'd sleep for a couple of hours, along with everyone else in Italy. At four o'clock every afternoon, the people of Padua roused themselves to pour into the streets and piazzas, dressed in their finest, for passeggiata, or the afternoon stroll. The harsh temperatures of the day sweetened into fresh breezes that carried aromas from the restaurants and take-out shops that opened their doors to entice the crowds. We would go out for a bite to eat and sit on a wooden bench under the arcades to busk and watch the crowds. Girls passed with their dark hair fluffed up and miniskirts hugging their hips. Eyes flashing, a dash of pink on pouting lips, they strolled onto the piazza in laughing groups, casually oblivious to the attention they attracted. Their male counterparts strove to cultivate an attitude of disinterest.

The Petrucchi Café, just a few blocks from our hotel, was a famous watering hole for everyone who was anyone in Padua for centuries, and Charlie found himself drawn to that neo-Classical masterpiece for its unobtrusive service, air conditioning, and dirt-cheap whiskey. He spent hours sitting at a corner pretending to be a turn-of-the-century wastrel squandering the family money. Terry started hanging out with a student at the university who sold him pot. Pete and I were determined to rise above our hand-to-mouth predicament, and struggled to maintain a vigorous busking schedule.

One implacable wall we rammed into early was the problem of meeting girls. We never had any difficulties north of the Alps, but in Italy, language wasn't the only barrier. We weren't Italian. Their families didn't know our families. We wore jeans and appeared to have lower standards of grooming. The girls we ran into liked our music, found us momentarily entertaining, but ultimately they decided that we were strange and a little scary. Pete formed a theory that their grandmothers remembered how many pregnant Italian girls were left in the wake of the American army during the war, and frightened their granddaughters with tales of our fertility.

One Paduan who liked us without reservation was a homeless alcoholic named Frank who staggered up to cheer us on every time we played. "Play your music for the people, Charlie!" he cried out, holding up a half-empty wine bottle. "Charlie, play your flute for the people!" Afterwards he would offer to take our passports to an unspecified location for safekeeping. To his perpetual disappointment, we never took him up on the offer. Pete laughed at him every time he tried. "Your friend Peter is too rough," Frank would mutter to me. "He is too rough."

A side effect of busking through Europe was that we didn't see the places we visited through the eyes of tourists—we were always looking to where we could make money. We all but ignored the tourist spots, preferring to go after the tourists themselves. We lived in a nether world between tourists and residents without being either. On the day we finally took the train to Venice, the place was heaving. The sun was hot and unrelenting, and the smell of dead fish from the canals overpowering. We busked for hours in several locations for the hordes, but the only money we made was one nickel grudgingly tossed into our hat by an American nun. One nickel. We couldn't spend it or even exchange it if we wanted to.

As summer eased into autumn, the locals began to view us with a concern that bordered on outright suspicion. The tourists returned home to work and school. Life in Padua resumed its centuries-old rhythm. We read the hints of curiosity everywhere-why were those long-haired English-speakers in their jeans and t-shirts still hanging around, still busking? Don't they have homes to go back to? Don't they know summer is over and everyone needs to go back to where they belong? Why won't they leave?

Eventually, those vibes began to get to us. The weather was getting cooler, and up north it would be soon be too cold to busk. We hoped to get gigs in Germany, and after being robbed once, we felt a little nervous being so far from London, where our open tickets allowed us to catch a flight home whenever we finally had to leave. However, when we found out that the big Padua wine festival was about to heave into action, we decided to stick around to pick up a few thousand last lira. Pete walked down to get us a gig on the festival stage, and as he usually did, he talked and talked until the organizer cried "Uncle" and surrendered a twenty minute slot just before midnight.

When I got to the Piazza del Santo on the night of the festival, Charlie and Terry were sitting glassy-eyed on a step in front of a wine shop. Pete hurried over with two girls in tow. "Here, I just met these lovely Irish girls," he said, flinging one arm over the blonde's shoulder. "This one's Angie. That's Marisa. They're on a work exchange program with a load of other Irish people."

Marisa's face was framed by walnut curls, and her green eyes were emerald flames. She was short and her body compact. If I saw her passing me on the street, I would have stopped and stared at her until she was out of view, and then mentally savored that image for the rest of the day. She looked me over once before latching onto my arm and leading me into the midst of the festival, peppering me with questions about our journeys. Shadows tumbled across the piazza, where rows of wine stands formed meandering walkways. Groups of revellers stood sampling the wines local vintners brought into town. At one end of the piazza, sound and light engineers rigged a large stage with lights and speakers. Strings of lights dangled from the trees and poles that surrounded the square, while the venerable Basilica glowed like a vast cluster of golden beehives in the sunset. Artificial lights flickered on as we entered the festival area, while people streamed in from capillary lanes feeding the piazza. We sat on the marble step of one of the shops on the square to watch the festival build up momentum.

During a lull in our conversation, Marisa suddenly clasped her hands around my neck, pulled down my head, and thrust her tongue into my mouth, nearly choking me as I reeled with astonishment. She rubbed her hands up and down my back, my head, everywhere, her tongue still darting over my teeth and gums, and straining for my uvula.

After I recovered from the shock, I responded in kind, and for several minutes we entwined ourselves together in the shadow of the grape shark. Then she broke free, panting hard. "I want to rape you," she gasped. She fixed me with a look that meant business, and enveloped my ear in her lips while my blood temperature shot up.

She slammed the right buttons, and I feverishly searched my mental map of the town for some park, alleyway, or bush we could retire to in order to resolve the situation. I already knew that Silvio wouldn't let her slip into my room. "Oh God, oh God!" We squeezed and caressed each other in the whirlpool of people.

"Marisa, maybe we should go somewhere else." Marisa clutched me with hot, undulating desire, but the fact that I hardly knew her made the situation feel so comical that I had to laugh. I couldn't help thinking that, for the first time, I might finally do what friends back home no doubt assumed I was doing all along. She attacked my mouth again with increased vigor, and her hands worked toward my nether regions like serpents inching toward their prey.

"Let's go find a nice bush somewhere." Passion was overwhelming the humor of the situation. I had had enough, and my hormones demanded serious action.

I felt a tap on my shoulder. "Come on, mate, we've got to play. We need this money. You can carry on with this later."

"Damn!" Throbbing, I reluctantly got up and followed Pete to the stage. Marisa kept one arm around my waist. As we walked, I felt a sore spot at the back of my throat. My sinuses sprang a series of leaks, and my head started to pound. My body felt hot and drained. I knew immediately that I was dealing with a serious flu. Ever since I was small, the symptoms attacked swiftly and without mercy. When I turned to look at that beautiful Irish girl with her dark, tumbling hair and emerald eyes filled with lust, I cursed the cruelty of fate. I'd be lucky to stay conscious for the next half hour. "Marisa, you'd better take some vitamin C."

It was a sorry-looking band that made its way onto the stage of the Padua wine festival-Charlie struggling to put his flute together, Terry with his glazed eyes and stoner grin, Pete with a frown, and me woozy with fever. Swirling spotlights bathed the crowd, and the roar of welcome that rose to greet us echoed and dissipated through all the streets, boulevards and alleyways of the ancient city. I blinked through the lights at the vast horde of Italians that stretched across the square. Then I glanced over at Marisa, who watched offstage shouting good-natured insults.

Terry lifted his fiddle to one microphone and flew into an impassioned set of reels. The crowd howled and I jumped back from the noise. Charlie bumbled over the first few notes before getting into a groove.

The crowd went crazy, stomping and clapping along with the tunes. People danced in circles, and some in the very front pounded their fists on the stage.

Miraculously, we made it through the first number without mishap. Before the applause let up, I launched into a jig. Our confidence renewed, we started to enjoy ourselves.

"Go for it, mate!" Pete shouted as he did a little dance of his own.

I heard the fiddle droning out of tune. Before I knew what was happening I stumbled backwards and landed hard on my rear end. As if on cue, Pete stopped playing and started swearing at me.

The audience clapped, but without much conviction. I felt too weak to get up, but Charlie staggered over to the microphone. "Thank you very much, ladies and gentlemen of this lovely city, where I have been rejected by a beautiful woman. Yes, but it is only what I deserved. So this one is for my lost and only love, who captured my heart, marinated it in vinegar, roasted it over a fire of thorns, stomped all over it with cleated boots, and handed it back to me in a plastic bag without so much as a rubber band to close it properly. Now I require only two things more. Fresh horses and more whiskey!" He tottered forwards, backwards, and collapsed.

The moon peered over the domes and towers of the basilica while Pete dragged us off the stage with a string of profanity so ornate and intensely felt that I nearly cried.

"These two are useless," I heard Marisa tell Angie as I tried to stand up. I watched with watering eyes as they disappeared into the crowd, feeling despair and relief at the same time. No discussion was required at that point. We had long outworn our welcome, and after that farewell performance, we couldn't be out of there fast enough. I started to understand how Galileo must have felt.

Silvio stood waiting in his bathrobe at the hotel, his hair dishevelled and his hands on his hips. As we filed despondently in, he tapped at his watch. "I tell you, meed-a-night, meed-a-night! Where you are? We close! Do not you hear?"

He calmed down considerably when Pete paid him and the rest of us grabbed our belongings and dragged them downstairs into the lobby. "You leave now, yes? Okay, you leave. Goodbye."

Several hours later we pulled over on the road up to the St. Gotthard Pass to watch the pink fingers of dawn touch the tops of the Alps. The ache of hunger stirred in my stomach. The air was chilly, and we dug deep into our packs to find sweaters and jackets for the long, long road ahead.

# The Corridors of Power

*Clare Glennon*

Michael Stirling was heading back to his office, sucking a mint to disguise the smell of his mid morning cigarette. He veered to the right of the corridor, superstitiously keeping as far away as possible from the conference room. As he passed by the door opened and two men came out in mid conversation. The older man wore a crisp shirt, his identity badge tucked into his top pocket. The other was more casual, short sleeves and jeans. They looked vaguely familiar – I.T. guys, perhaps.

"I'm not blaming you, cos you're just a menial."

"I'm lower than a snake's belly, me."

Michael wondered at the cheerful satisfaction in the men's voices. Guess they don't have a new mortgage and a wife who's eight weeks pregnant, he thought bitterly.

At his desk, Michael contemplated the photo stuck with blutack to the edge of his computer. Him and Angie, on the beach last year, making silly faces at the camera. He hadn't told her. Not yet. Nothing was definite yet, anyway.

Michael looked up at the large clock on the wall, even though the time showed clearly on the screen of his PC and on his watch. Chris followed his gaze.

"Almost high noon."

Michael couldn't reply. He had recruited Chris personally, six months before. He ought to appreciate the attempt at gallows humour, he knew, but no words came into his head. He wondered if he had time for a visit to the toilet, then remembered. He had just come back from there, ten minutes before. With a quick decision he spun his chair round, got up and walked out of his office.

The conference room was dominated by a wall-mounted screen. Acting Chief of Operations (U.K.) John Raymond stood to one side, casually tapping a laser pointer into the palm of his hand. No meeting of Raymond's was complete without a power point presentation. He did not acknowledge Michael. On the screen the company logo tumbled up and down and across, like a lifeless body in the sea.

Ten minutes later and the room was full. As the other managers filed in, not one of them caught Michael's eye.

Raymond moved to the centre. He introduced the trio from Head Office with a flourish, earning a nod from one of them at the flawless pronunciation of their German names.

In solemn tones, Raymond outlined the current situation. Falling revenues, poor economic climate, underperformance from certain key departments.

After the last comment he turned quickly back to the screen, as if from a sense of delicacy.

"Bastard." Michael thought.

The sales team had 'again' failed to secure a vital contract, losing out to Millennium, their main competitor. Raymond was facing the room once more. He gave a little shrug.

"Perhaps we should ask Millennium, 'What's your secret?'"

Two of the men from Stuttgart frowned. This was not a time for levity. Michael felt an absurd rush of gratitude.

It still didn't make sense. The sales team had worked for months. Late nights, early mornings and endless bitter coffee from the staff canteen. Their research was insanely detailed. Michael would swear that his team knew the layout of Hopkins plc better than their own homes. Millennium could not possibly have done better. The rival company hadn't spent the money and they hadn't put in the work. Arriving at the last minute and undercutting their bid made no sense at all.

Raymond quickly brought up a new screen. Three yellow words on a blue background. *The Way Forward*.

Everyone in the room already knew the proposal. Shut down the British operation as a going concern. Leave a staff of a dozen or so to service existing clients and liaise with Germany. Axe everyone else. Retain one of the department heads to oversee it all. Not too many Indians, but one big new chief. Raymond sighed, as if pained. Michael saw Johnson from R & D and Danny Khan from Finance exchange a bitter glance. No guessing who the new top man would be. Raymond straightened, as if saddened but resolute, and clicked to change the screen.

Michael didn't know what he was seeing, at first. A photograph, a little dark, a little grainy, but clear enough. Two men at a restaurant table. A table crowded with the remains of a meal: crockery, glasses and a white A4 envelope, bulging. On the left Michael recognised Simon Wright, the Head of Sales at Millennium. To the right, leaning back, gesturing with a large cigar, sat John Raymond.

A bright red dot trembled at the edge of a brandy glass, then slid down the screen. Raymond held his fist to his stomach, the laser pointer drooping. His face was white. His mouth opened once, then closed.

Absolute silence. One of the men from Stuttgart stood up. He addressed the room, his accent giving a strange sense of formality to his words.

"Ladies, gentlemen, this meeting is adjourned."

No one looked at anyone else as they filed out of the conference room, as if in unspoken agreement they were waiting to be outside before exploding into talk. As Michael approached the door his eye caught a tucked in I.D. card, a crisp white shirt and he looked up. The man was smiling past him. As Michael turned, he heard the low voice of a younger man just to his right.

"Yup. Lower than a snake's belly."

# Strike up the Band

*Virginia Moffatt*

I see him every morning, when I step out of the house to get the milk. Every morning at seven o'clock. Sometimes it's ten past, I don't always get out of bed on time these days. Every day he smiles, "Good morning," before taking his head off with his bare hands, whilst behind him the fiery sun explodes through the clouds. His mouth is open in, laughter? Rage? I'm never quite sure. He does it long enough to know I have seen him, the neckless head, the headless neck. Then he places it back, says 'I'm feeling light headed today,' or some other smart alec remark and walks away. It is no use trying to trick him, to stay in bed, to refuse to go out. If I don't make it to the door, he enters the house, does his little turn and leaves me to face up to the day ahead.

The faceless men are always there to observe our morning encounters. They stand grey-headed on the opposite side of the street. Their featureless bodies not entirely dreary, on account of the colour of their suits. I've been seeing them every day for weeks now, but it still never ceases to intrigue me, why, when everything else is uniform, they choose to dress this way. There's Mr Tartan, with his red and black squares. Next to him, Mr Flower Power, in his mustard-suit adorned in bold florals - pink, blue, red and white. Last of all, Mr Stripes dressed in irregular diagonals - greens, reds, yellows, oranges, a surprise of purple. They never speak, but sing an early morning chorus:

*Let the drums roll out,*
*Let the trumpet call,*
*While the people shout, 'Strike up the band!'*

I have stopped shouting at them to shut up, it upsets the neighbours. It upsets my wife, who asks me why in God's name I am standing on the doorstep yelling nonsense again. So I go back inside, the song ringing in my head. I take the milk to the fridge as my wife doles out the assignments necessary for the smooth running of Operation School-run. When all are fed and watered; have lunchtime provisions; all teeth are clean; shoes polished fit for a sergeant-major - I dispatch my family in the four by four, and I can leave the house to go to the job I am supposed to attend each day.

The job I am supposed to attend each day, but have ceased to attend for several weeks now. My wife doesn't know. She must never find out. Every morning as she takes the children off, I dutifully walk down the road to the train station. I am always pursued by my grey-faced, colourfully-suited choir.

*There is work to be done, to be done,*
*Let's have fun, fun, fun,*
*Come on son of a gun, gun, gun, take your stand!*

I take the train as I am supposed to, but only for two stops. At Southend Central, I get out and walk through the back streets, coming down the hill by Never Never Land in the cliff gardens. I used to play there once, before the cliff falls and the vandals, in a time when every nook and cranny spelt adventure. Now there are keep out signs, the paint is peeling off the play-houses and I don't want an adventure ever again. As I reach the pier, my grey men are singing from their mouth-less faces with gusto,

*Form a line oh, oh,*
*Come on, let's go*
*Hey leader, 'strike up the band!'*

I suppose I don't mind them really. Some days I even quite like their singing. It gives me something to hum along to, so I don't have to worry about anything else. About the fact that I am not at work. About the fact that I stopped going sometime ago, around the time my friend with the detachable head arrived. Around the time my personal choir started following me around. So I sing along as I start out down the pier, the tune beating my path over the creaking boards out to sea. Through the cracks between the wood, I can see the water deepening from the brown, muddy shallows, to the green swirly depths where the motorboats launch. The wind strengthens its grip on me. By the time I reach the end of the railway line, the water is grey-green, the air sea-fresh. Of course, since the fire, there's not much to see out here: the burnt out buildings of two-thousand and five, adding to the blackened timbers of the previous fires further on out to sea. Only the lifeboat station has survived the latest conflagration intact – still on hand to rescue those in need. I'm not sure there's any salvation for someone as lost at me, but I like to sit here, tucked in a corner, out of the wind. I like watching the fishermen and the large ships going up and down the estuary.

Sometimes, I pretend I'm on board a ship, far out to sea, a long way from home. It's better than staying at home, at any rate, sitting with my memories.

It doesn't do any good to remember. It leads me to places I'd rather not be. Places where I was sent by the grey faceless men. The men who make all the decisions without ever living through the consequences. The faceless men who send others into war zones, they would never dare enter themselves. Like the convoy on the way to the Christmas Panto. Andy, Pat and Dean dressed as clowns in their tartan, floral, stripy suits, wearing silly noses and making daft jokes. Alec, smart Alec, not so smart that day, poking his head out of the side of the Humvee we borrowed from the Yanks. Alec, smart Alec, not so smart that day, whose head was lifted right of his neck. A headless neck, a neckless head, as the roadside bomb exploded beside our truck and we were sent helter skelter, and all the while on the radio I could hear the sound of singing:

*Form a line, oh, oh*
*Come on, let's go*
*Hey, Mr. Leader,*
*Hey, Mr. Leader,*
*Please 'strike up the band!'*

# The Entrails

*Muhammad Ashfaq*

Since an extra one hundred thousand bucks was by way of a sheer windfall and had never been a factor in the decision-making equation, they reckoned they were fully justified in celebrating it.

She dressed up both of the boys to the kill i.e. the best available clothing, but herself had to be put up with the common attire; she had none else. Hardly any debate was required as to what would be the merriment like; both Ali and Wali had been clamoring to go to McDonalds for a long time for a full meal, that is, something beyond morsels and left-over drops of Coca Cola. Allah Ditta could never – despite his best efforts – manage enough to fulfil their cherished dream; necessities always availed primacy over the luxuries.

Today they could afford it; Allah Ditta was no more though. -

"Hey, you can't enter the hall!" The doorman standing by McDonalds probably recognized them.

Wali – the younger of the two – in his excitement, was already behind the glass-door. One of the guards rushed to get him off his neck.

"You don't dare put your hands on my child!" Wali's mother, in her feeble and pitiable voice growled at the guard. She looked scruffy in her mid-thirties; the ruins revealed that the edifice must have been splendid.

Before both sides could get into act, the people around intervened and controlled the situation. They returned with a shattered dream pining and whining. Although their hearts were all into it, yet the forces of nature were conspiring to defeat their valued dream. On the way back she bought them *Nan Pakora* from a roadside cart, and they were home again.

The same night second tragedy befell the family within a fortnight.

Allah Ditta, like his sons, had too been orphaned at a young age. His mother had died when he was twelve, and father, a village drummer by profession, left him at fourteen. By that time, he had dropped out of the school having been consistently beaten by the village schoolteacher. A paternal uncle, upon his father's death, rightfully assumed the responsibility, and deposited him in a close-by Maktab – the ultimate abode of orphans and near-orphans.

Maktab had sprung only a few years ago just a couple of miles from the village, but made a pacey progress. From outside, it did not look like a school but a mini fort – a huge complex in the midst of agri-fields with a two hundred meter kacha access to the pucca road that led to the border town. Crudely cemented brick walls on all four sides gave the complex a mysterious and unpleasant look. The gate was iron-plated with razor-sharp spikes fixed on top of it, and was guarded round the clock by the turban-wearing stick-bearing youth. Inside, it had long straight halls cut into sections for different grades. Level one was fully reserved for residence purposes with no windows opening outside but inside the compound. There was a mess too – operated under the supervision of one of the two deputies to Maktab Chief. The other deputy looked after the accounts, charity and other funds.

Allah Ditta was kept and fed well at Maktab; his good looks further galvanized. He was taught Arabic, Persian, and Urdu, and the basics of religion. He was also trained in piety and made to offer his prayers regularly. His heart was not much into it but felt his life here was better than that before when he was most of the times hungry. He made friends with Haq Nawaz – a stout and sombre-looking senior student-cum-faculty member. Haq Nawaz himself was under-training in oration, law, and other advanced disciplines; but also taught basic Tradition and elementary grammar to junior grades. They remained together for long hours studying, reading, tickling each other, and playing in leisure time; which used to be in short supply though.

Otherwise, Haq Nawaz being the chief-whip was an awe-inspiring creature within the environs of Maktab. He could ruthlessly beat the chained pupils with bamboo rods. It was an ordinary norm that the students who ran away and brought back by their parents or heirs were fettered with iron chains. The mere spectre of Haq Nawaz letting loose on deviants and absconders was quite a deterrent against nurturing of any notions of a life beyond Maktab boundary walls. Haq Nawaz was also in-charge of the workshop in the cellar of Maktab. He would go there in routine to oversee the work after punishing the delinquents. A couple of times, Allah Ditta was also favoured with a sneak into that otherwise out-of-bound section. He learned that in the cellar fireworks were prepared for the pupils. Shab-e-Barat came and passed, but neither he nor anyone else got firecrackers to enjoy. -

Maktab Chief – though gave his class no regular lessons, yet it was common knowledge that he had written over hundred treatises on waging holy war. This was his area of specialization and his natural eloquence and oration went well with the explosive and fiery subject. During Friday sermons he would engender awe in the hearts of his enemies – none could guess who they were, but some invisible and ethereal enemy was omni-present in the very ambience of Maktab. The brutalities being committed against the brethren across the globe were the main butt of his verbal attacks. He would extensively dilate upon the enormous need, the uncountable bounties associated with, and the superiority of this particular article of faith.

It was dreary for Allah Ditta that Maktab Chief would repeatedly perform the same particular Verses, and then delve deep into their hair-splitting interpretations. He would recapitulate with his favorite punchline: "Murder has been made obligatory upon you, Brothers!" Allah Ditta had seen deaths of his parents in tender age and the sermons of death and destruction would send shivers down his backbone.

This was potent and pervasive indoctrination – although against an equally rough and unabsorbing terrain. Allah Ditta felt increasing repulsion and dissonance deep down in his heart. He was afraid. He wanted to live.

Many a times he felt like talking it out with Haq Nawaz, but he really was not sure how he would react. Their bond was yet to be put to a test. He thought, he planned, he chickened out many a times over. He was not afraid of escaping; he was afraid of getting caught and brought back all fours tied.

One day, however, Allah Ditta escaped from Maktab – for good – leaving behind a note for Haq Nawaz.

He did not return to the village; none there awaited him. He went to the city. He roamed around for days searching food, shelter, and job, but did not dare go to a mosque – was afraid of getting spotted. He nurtured notions to become a helper, a conductor, a cleaner, a mason, or a waiter at a hotel, but since none knew him, none trusted him, none hired him. So he could never manage for the next day.

During the initial few months, he slept on the footpath, but then he found his accommodation under the bridge of now shrivelled river Ravi. Soon he also covered one of the two open sides of the compartment, and transformed it into a room by putting a door on it.

In leisure hours, it became his favorite pastime to stand up the bridge and observe trucks, cars, carts, and pedestrians cross the Ravi Bridge. He had a keen eye, and he would love watching vultures hovering over the river in clear blue skies. These vultures had gathered slowly as the rich people crossing the bridge in their expensive cars would throw them meat as charity of their bounties. Looking at the starved and stunted children of his under-the-bridge community, he would ponder long and hard about these vulture-feeding people.

Many a times he wished he were a vulture.

Thinking it was inconvenient for the rich people to go and buy meat for the vultures, he ended up inventing a new profitable vocation for himself. One morning, he went to the near-by butcher shop and collected the entrails thrown out of the shop in a polythene bag, stood on the Ravi Bridge, and sold them. Next day the butcher also gratefully cooperated. It then became his routine. In the morning, he would diligently collect innards from all butcher shops in the outer city area, stand up the bridge to sell them for good money by the mid-day. He loved the sight of waiting vultures plucking the falling shards of meat mid-air. It was both pleasure and profession for him. At sundown, he sat on the hut-hotel by the roadside, read newspaper, and leisurely sipped tea.

Life was not supposed to be that simple and dull for him. One day he met up Rani – a stray woman – who had eloped with her paramour from a far off village. The man ditched her in Lahore, and ran with her jewellery and money that she had fetched with from her parents' home. As she was scared of going back to her home and getting killed, Allah Ditta purposely chaperoned her to his under-the-bridge home. Haq Nawaz was on the call of duty to solemnize their marriage a week later.

Rani gave birth to two beautiful sons before falling prey to breast cancer to keep it eventful.

The government hospital recommended chemotherapy for which they had no money. Initially they managed it through painkillers, but then Cancer started living in the home like fifth member of the family; most of the times the most important one.

Allah Ditta realized that the profession he innovated was now turning into an industry as more and more people surfaced on the scene with entrails bags. The butchers now also started to sell their previously useless by-product. A serious dent in his revenues was the result.

On the other hand, Rani's health started deteriorating symptomized by extreme pain, lack of appetite, and sleeplessness. Reduced income coupled with increased expenditure, the boys now eight and six started feeling the pinch of starvation. Sometimes, he would send them to deputize for him and sell the entrails bags, but they were too young and tender, and the competition was fierce.

Things were getting slowly out of his control. He could not even get his haircut and shave done for a few months, about which he had been quite particular ever since escaping from Maktab. More painful, of course, was Rani's condition; chemotherapy was required and quickly.

One Tuesday morning (cutting of animals was banned on Tuesdays and Wednesdays), he took Rani and the boys to the main public transport junction, found an eventful nook, wrote and displayed the placard: "Save mother of two flower-like sons!" The accounts revealed a total return of seventeen rupees for the day. While rolling back their old rug that the family owned for an asset, he muttered unto himself: "Who the hell thought beggars were rich fellows, and earned more than the daily labourers!" The entire earnings went into purchase of cough syrup for Ali, bread for the family to be eaten with onions, and painkillers for Rani.

They tried their luck by visiting the government hospital again. The doctor while prescribing on a piece of paper an expensive painkiller to be bought from a druggist, advised them to start chemotherapy without any further delay.

Sitting on the hut-hotel, a sea of thoughts went through his mind. Suddenly, there was a glimmer in his eyes. The newspaper in his hands carried a story that a distraught man had put his kids for sale and because of the hype created by the media, the President, the Prime Minister, and the Governor had scrambled to help him; he was offered the job of a sweeper in the municipality. He went running down the bridge to share it with Rani.

Next morning leaving ailing Rani back home, he took both of the boys to another busy roadside point, and displayed the banner: "Sons for Sale". To his utter surprise, nobody noticed the placard; nobody took him seriously. A few times, looking at his merchandize he broke into tears.

About mid-day, the area police inspector Khushi Muhammad conducted raid, and stuffed all of them into the back-cabin of police van along with their rug and the placard, and sped away. "I am sick of you paupers, and your antics", said Khushi Muhammad while nudging him in the midsection with his bamboo hand-stick at the police station. After receiving both verbal and physical thrashing from Khushi Muhammad, when they reached back home late that night they found their woman in agonizing pain. They had no money that night to buy her painkillers.

This was a terrible night; terrible enough to make terrible decisions.

When the boys were gone to sleep after having one-half bread each with onion, the man and wife without much deliberation on the matter decided to go into the fold of eternal peace collectively. They loved their sons and did not want to leave them behind to die of hunger.

"What could be the easiest method?" Rani asked distractedly.

"I don't know. It's my first attempt!" He replied curtly. "But I think poison should be the least painful."

"Ok, then tomorrow?" She asked emerging from an excruciatingly painful condition.

"Are you finally decided?" He enquired expectantly.

"Yes." Clarity of head had been her hall-mark all life.

"Do we have money to get it?" Allah Ditta questioned unwantingly.

"I have five rupees, and you?" She said without budging an inch, and forcefully communicating her resolve.

"May be the same amount." He started crying and kissing Wali who was sleeping beside him.

"They are a blessing of Allah. Let's not be thankless while returning His blessings back to Him..." She kissed Ali, and started coughing which was to go on for a while. Apart from Rani's sporadic coughing and trucking sound over the bridge, a sinisterly silence prevailed in the darkness; none knew who went to sleep when.

The next afternoon when Allah Ditta returned, instead of rat-kill pills, he carried newspaper in his hands – again.

"I have an idea – a real good one." He said rather soberly.

"What?" She asked coughing and disappointedly.

"There was a bomb blast in Rawalpindi last week, and the government has announced compensation of one hundred thousand rupees for each one who died in the blast." She was dumb, expressionless, and cold. "You don't get it!" He said looking deep into her darkening eyes. "Why all four of us? Why my flower-like sons? Why you?" There was a lump in his throat. "It should be me only. You people would get enough money in compensation to get the treatment, the chemotherapy, and live comfortably. Then they would grow up and start doing something."

I don't know but...!" She could not complete her sentence, but he got she was enquiring about the execution plan. He was little depressed; Rani had agreed to the proposition without any fuss.

"I think I can manage it." He said and retired.

A day later, he returned fully equipped with a cummerbund after meeting Haq Nawaz. The plan was that he would blow himself up to cause mayhem, and the rest would be close-by enough to claim the casualty.

Allah Ditta kissed his sons, half-hugged Rani, shed a few drops, wiped his eyes, kept his cool, walked a few hundred yards, turned back to have a last look at his family, and blew himself up with a bang in the midst of bustling Yadgar Chowk; it was a perfectly executed deed. The final count was seventeen dead, and twenty-two seriously injured. The human innards including those of Allah Ditta were splayed all over the place. For a while, the boys thought to gather them for the next day's business but then all were scrambling for life. Soon countless vultures were hovering over the sight as if to commemorate the death of their benefactor.

The family's presence on the scene helped and they were registered as legitimate heirs to one of the victims of the tragedy.

They returned home late rather unconcerned as to what had happened just hours ago, and that their fourth member was not with them that night. No one talked on the way.

After a week they came to know that the Governor had announced a compensation package of one hundred thousand rupees for the families of the dead, and fifty thousand rupees for each of the injured.

They received the compensation money in a green envelope a week later. Haq Nawaz visited them and informed that the President had also announced an additional compensation of one hundred thousand rupees for them and that they would soon receive the same. While departing, he lovingly caressed and cajoled the boys.

Suddenly they forgot the tragedy – the very source of all the blessings, and felt themselves to be on the moon. In particular, the additional one hundred thousand rupees was totally unexpected, and they decided to celebrate the occasion by having a dinner at McDonalds – the boys' ultimate dream.

They could not, however, and had to buy *Nan Pakora* from a roadside cart on their way back.

They were still finishing their dinner, when Khushi Muhammad violently barged into their candle-lit room with his men armed to the teeth.

For a moment they thought the second green envelope had also arrived.

Khushi Muhammad told Rani that the latest investigations had revealed that Allah Ditta was not a victim but a perpetrator of the catastrophe.

Her face remained usual expressionless; speechless.

When they took Rani out of the room for further investigations along with the green packet, she turned back and had a last look at her sons – their faces were expressionless, too. Just a couple of tears rolled down the younger one's cheeks.

Next morning, Haq Nawaz came and took the flower-like sons to Maktab.

# Time To Go

*Simon Kellow-Bingham*

I had a headache. A really bad stress headache and my co-worker Bundy was not helping. He was scratchy and up for a faux gangsta banter and today, of all airport days, I could really do without his juvenile street script. The lights in the office flickered. My laptop pinged. My workbag was fat beneath my desk. I rubbed my eyes.

"I think I have a brain tumour."
"What? Are you crazy?"
"I have trouble seeing and I have bad headaches all day long."
"Check your age man. You is middle-aged already."
"No. I'm younger than that. It must be a tumour."
"Vanity is a sin man."
"What are you talking about Bundy?"
"Is you going deaf too? Get your ass to an optician."

I was sure I had seen the sign on the desk at reception this morning warning of a fire alarm test. I checked my mobile phone. I had to hold it at arm's length before the numbers were really clear enough to read. Too much reflection. It was ten-forty-five. Tests were at ten on a Friday, every Friday. They never do it twice in one day. This wasn't déjà vu. This was real. Time to go.

"This fire exit has taken us airside."
"So you is not as dumb as you look?"
"I don't look as dumb as you. This is a restricted zone. You don't have a pass."
"Neither does you tumour-boy."
"How will we get back?"
"Just wait by the fire exit. The fireman will call us back in,"
"Okay."
"Hey man, that's the bag you bring in to work."
"No. Not mine."

Baggage trucks dash past our office window several times an hour on busy days. It's not unusual to see a bag spill off the stack now and then. They say the drivers are trained not to stop and only go back if instructed. I saw a nice expensive looking bag get run over last week. I would hate that to happen to mine.

"Is that the Fire Truck?"
"I see no smoke bro'-"
"I saw fireworks last night."
"Kids been setting them down my street since October. No-one waits for the fifth of November in my yard no more innit?"

"Can you smell anything?"
"Not me. You is the only thing I can smell!"
"Nice."
"Man, is you sure that ain't your bag?"

A baggage truck pulled up next to the offending bag. The driver stepped down and hefted it into the stack on his trailer. I guess it was pretty heavy for a small bag. I looked away. A fireman arrived at the exit door and waved us back into the building.

"At least it wasn't raining."
"True, big storms coming across laters."
"I heard it was a Panini."
"Say what?"
"It set off the alarm."
"A sandwich? You shittin' me?"
"The Atrium Cafe does toasties Bundy, yeah?"
"Ah. Right."
"I think it was a tuna melt."

At lunchtime I went out to Go-Glasses, the express spectacle shop in the mall. I thought perhaps it was the sin of vanity and there was a chance my eyesight was dimming. Maybe it was just the massive stress I felt right now? Perhaps I just needed some sleep? It turned out that the girl at the opticians was the optician. Did that mean I really was getting old?

"Sorry?"
"I just need to shine a light in your eyes."
"I wondered why you were so close to me."
"Excuse me sir?"
"I never had an eye exam before."
"I won't bite."

"No. It's just I ate spring onions before I got here,"
"Oh, I see."
"I'll hold my breath."
"Thanks now look up."

I stopped to check out my reflection in the window of an electrical store. I looked pretty cool in my new frames, or was that me being vain? God knows we all have our weak spots. I checked out the wall of televisions on display in the shop window and noticed a TV presenter with similar eyewear. I was on trend.

"Check me out. I can see."
"Nice man. You'll see loads of fireworks in those tonight."
"You looking out for a show later?"
"There's a massive storm system pushing in off the Atlantic, remains of some sweet girlie named tropical hurricane. She gonna steal your roof."
"So more rain?"
"Yup! I'll be watching any fireworks on my new Three-Dee television."
"Three-Dee, huh. Go to the theatre Bundy."
"You off home eye-boy?"
"Sure."
"Don't forget your bag man."
"Thanks, but I didn't bring it in today. I travel light on a Friday."

I went back to the mall to get my frames adjusted at Go-Glasses. I peered in at the electrical store window. The news was on and the reporter was wearing my specs. I could easily read the ticker at the bottom of the screen. A seven-four-seven was missing over the

Atlantic. I thought I might just go out and watch some fireworks tonight after all.

# Being Twenty-One

*JF Chavoor*

It was dark, even for a bar. But that was ok, that was good, that hid me as well as it hid her. I was drinking Wild Turkey on the rocks, or Seven and Seven or gin and tonic because those were the only drinks I could call out and not sound foolish. I wasn't having beer though. Beer was recreational, to relax and laugh. Beer 'took the edge off' as I heard so many people say when I got a little older. All I knew at the time was beer took off, or erased or smoothed over my angry dad, my underachieving, underwhelming grades, my silly sense of style and coolness, along with my cowardice, fears, insecurity, dishonesty and almost complete unawareness of anything and everything regarding my life, the immediate world around me, the larger world and myself and my relationship to people, school, work, bars, drinks, faith and cynicism. Once all that was evaporated with the first sip of beer, then I could be free and move about and speak, laugh and enjoy life unencumbered. There were occasions when I got drunk, but I had no need to because everything I needed was in that first sip; in that moment it felt as though my soul exhaled after holding its breath for much longer than it should have. I mostly got drunk only if I wasn't paying for it. It seemed to me at the time somehow less stupid to get drunk if it was at someone else's expense. I wasn't a complicated kid; it would be doubly stupid to a) get drunk and b) spend money to accomplish the goal. At a party or a beer bust in a dorm at least it wasn't my own parent-funded dough.

But this wasn't beer, this was Wild Turkey, or Seagram's or any old generic gin, it was a different set of circumstances. Drinking liquor, knowing the names of drinks, drinking the drink, recognizing the flavor of the drink and being familiar with it—these were all things that I was young enough to believe made me look older, which is to say made me look like I had lived a life without having lived one, and it was something done not at all consciously, but innately, with the same instincts that drive every 21 year old to declare and express his individuality by dressing just like every other 21 year old in a particular corner of the world in a particular time period, deep inside the bowels of a particular zeitgeist. At the time it was a leisure suit, a puka shell necklace, bathed liberally in any current aftershave which made you smell like a candy store, two-tone shoes, and the hair was to be styled by a stylist, not merely cut by a barber. I bought it all. I wasn't entirely or even remotely enamored with any of it but it was the ticket for admission and I wanted in. I was jazzed, elated, overjoyed that I was entering the world, that I was in the world and the world was in me, regardless of what my church and Sunday school teachers told me; I knew there had to be a little of both—heaven and the world—in order to human enough to be spiritual, and it didn't bother me in the least that I looked ridiculous in a brown leisure suit.

I wasn't dressed the night I met the girl I knew nothing about. I was out of uniform, well, I was in my day uniform—sweatshirt, jeans, and tennies. Lenny and I were out just prowling around in the weather beaten '69 Chevelle with the bad muffler, the missing hubcap, the rust spot on the hood like an open wound, the radio that only worked occasionally, the smell of dirt, sweat, sunflower seeds and hormones, not to mention the broken glove box that regularly fell open, hitting me on the knee.

Lenny had heard of a party somewhere near Westwood. He had heard of it but didn't know who was hosting and we didn't know a single person there. He heard it from someone who knew someone. Maybe he overheard it, I don't know. But Lenny always functioned best when his mind was running one way, focused on the target, like he was engaged in some unnamed, unknown sport that required intense, singular concentration. We were going to this party of Polo shirts and Porsches and that was that. I didn't want to go, wasn't interested in going, even if I had the clothes and the car. Even if I knew some of the people there, I still wasn't interested. But I wasn't driving, I never drove and that seemed to preclude any input on my part regarding where we were going and what we were doing. We got there, got stared at, got spoken to in snarky tones and headed back to the car before we even made it to the front door.

We were purged, cast off, sent packing. We drifted off in the unsightly Chevelle, moving away from Sunset Boulevard as if it were to blame. Lenny went east, then north. We were silent while the radio faded in, then out, then in again. Eventually Lenny spoke, choosing a topic as far away from our fiasco as possible. He explained that Bob Dylan, Paul Simon, and Leonard Cohen were great because they were Jewish.

"What about Neil Diamond? He sucks." I said.

"Yeah, right. He sucks so bad he's a millionaire ten times over."

"What about Neil Young, Joni Mitchell, Lennon and McCartney?"

"What about 'em?"

"They're great but they're not Jewish."

He didn't answer but instead abruptly flipped a u-turn.

"What are you doing?"

"We're going in there."

And that's how I ended up in the bar. I lost track of Lenny, ordered hard liquor instead of beer and met Mary from Mount St. Mary's. I couldn't see her, couldn't gain insights into who she was by her voice because the music was so loud I couldn't hear the tone, modulation or nuances. And it was dark but not a foreboding dark, just a plain, run of the mill dark that was darker than most bars I had been in. I didn't know where we were, didn't know the name of the bar, and Mary from Mount St. Mary's may not have been the girl on that particular night because that name was tossed around for a long time after Lenny and I first heard it, just for purposes of amusement. Mary from Mount St. Mary's might have been that night that Lenny drank peppermint schnapps and tried to hurdle a bush, failed miserably and either bruised or cracked a few ribs in the process. It might not have been Mary at all, it might have been another different night involving that Armenian girl who seemed unimpressed or even remotely interested with the fact that that out of a roomful of unknown odars (non Armenians) I was Armenian and we found each other. I began to doubt that she was even Armenian. How could she have been? We are a crazy, elated, enraged, people full of life, with strong disparate convictions. But this girl was deflated and nearly motionless. There was no life in her, as a matter of fact life had been kicking the crap out of her and she had this sense of defeat and humiliation that was so strong that not buying her a drink was not enough; I felt obliged to have her write down her number on a cocktail napkin and then tell her I wasn't going to call. She accepted this as the norm. She looked and acted as though her friends had talked her into this talking to strangers in a bar and she thought it was idiotic and was doing it against her will. It was idiotic to me as well but I was doing it gleefully, wholeheartedly, enthusiastically. It was part of being 21. If this was the game to play then I would play it and later, when I was old and mature and responsible I would remember my 21st year in the world and all the idiotic, wonderfully foolish things I had done.

But the girl in the bar didn't know any of that. She was already drunk when I found her, so while we sat on the barstools trying to talk, I waited for a slow song to invite her to dance. I was going to do everything and nothing and it would be fantastic and very, very foolish. When *Ballroom Blitz* ended, Art

Garfunkel's dreamy version of *I Only Have Eyes for You* poured out like molasses. I leaned close so she could see me nod my head in the direction of a glass panelled door that led to a small patio outside. I knew exactly what I was doing and I had absolutely no clue whatsoever. And so we danced.

There was no dance in the dance though, no touch to the touch, no souls glowing together. In Armenian you could say 'Pon chee ga,' or nothing there. There was nothing; it was less than nothing, that's all. But I wasn't going to let nothingness get in the way. I only had to get her attention.

"This is a great version of the song. It buries the original."

It was a completely reasonable thing to say to someone I didn't know, wouldn't know and wouldn't care if—when she got over her hangover late in the afternoon the next day—she had no memory of me. I looked at her while we danced without dancing. She looked left, right, to the floor, like parts of her were falling off, all very slowly, slower than the pace of the song that was too slow, even for slow dancing. I was thinking "though she feels as though she's in a play, she is anyway." She looked at me for a second; apparently temporarily forgetting that someone was in close proximity with his arms around her waist. She wasn't alarmed though and she readied her face to speak.

"Mmmurff."

Which I took to mean, "Why don't you kiss me already," so I did.

"Idina glergum," she said, a little more assertively than whatever it was she had just said the moment before.

I never understood a single word she said but my eyes were opened and I immediately felt ashamed and relieved. The song ended and we walked back into the bar, to our barstools, stood by our barstools saying nothing, thinking nothing or maybe saying simple niceties and thinking everything. It was a time of testing yourself against the prototypes of the day. I may not have known who I was at the time but in that moment I knew who I wasn't. We looked at each other and somehow became unacquainted strangers again, and I walked away as if I were just passing by anyone, any stranger in a bar that was darker than usual. I didn't worry about her, in a hour I wouldn't think or talk about her, and I had no doubt that she wouldn't remember much of anything, maybe someone she couldn't see or understand, saying something, hanging around for a while and then walking away. I went to find Lenny and we headed for the parking lot. He didn't get anywhere and when I told him my story he just laughed. It was drizzling rain but perspiration was rolling down the middle of my back. I peeled off my sweatshirt, flung it over my shoulder and stood in the middle of the parking lot taking in the cool, wet, night air. I felt good, felt alive, felt brand new.

"Come on, Jake, let's go," Lenny called as he got in the car.

"Ok, ok."

We found Sunset and headed to Hollywood to go up Highland to Barham and back to Burbank. I started singing quietly to myself.

"What the hell are you muttering?"

"A Dylan song."

"Which one?"

"And if anybody asks me, is it easy to forget? I'll say it's easily done just pick anyone and pretend that you never have met."

"It's not easy to do but you sing worse than Dylan."

"Shut up, man."

"Let's go to 7-11 and buy a six of Michelob."

"Sounds good."

By the time we passed Hollywood High we were far enough from L.A. and close enough to Burbank to feel like we were back home. The next morning I woke up with the story receding from the front of my head to the back; I was ready to move one day closer to being twenty-two.

## About The Authors

**JF Chavoor** I was born in Burbank, California where everyone thinks they have a screenplay in the works. But it wasn't always that way. When I was a kid, growing up the in the early 60's, Burbank was more like Mayberry, USA, dropped right in the middle of Babylon. There was Hollywood, not ten minutes away. We felt safe staying on our side, joining the Cub Scouts and playing for Park Leagues and riding bikes all over town. Wherever I've been, whatever I've experienced, the safe, square, corny life of Burbank, is deep in my soul, and it drives the stories I write. You can only write from the inside out, after all. I write because it beats watching TV and also because I want to preserve a lost world and I want to share that world with those who may miss it or may be too young to have experienced it.

**I John 4:7-8**

**Kathleen Doherty** of Parker, Colorado has had work published in *Foliate Oak*, *Hot Metal Press*, www.millionstories.net and *Metrosphere*, She is currently pursuing the bachelor's degree in English she forgot to get back in the seventies. She is also working fulltime, writing constantly and reading anything in front of her – including cereal boxes and pharmaceutical labels.


**Jemma Hathaway** is a svelte, successful and stylish thirty-one year old writer being held against her will in the body of a somewhat fleshy, reluctant customer service advisor, wearing sensible shoes! She hardly ever eats five-a-day, does not possess a crumb of common sense and credits her love of language to those bastions of her childhood; the quintessentially British and much lamented Ladybird books! She has recently obtained a First Class Honours in English Literature from The Open University and is now planning to undertake an MA in Creative Writing, and despite the fact that she should clearly be settled in a solid job with a stakeholder pension, a page-per-day calendar and the prospect of a cubic-zirconium-encrusted carriage clock by now, she remains indomitably optimistic that one day someone somewhere will consider paying her a few pennies to put her daydreams on to paper.

**Virginia Moffatt** was born in London, in 1965, one of eight children, including a twin sister who writes commercial fiction and an older sister who is a poet.

Virginia works for Oxfordshire County Council and lives in Oxford with her husband Chris and their three children. She has achieved a Diploma in Creative Writing at Oxford University Department of Continuing Education and attended a Faber Academy Weekend Course in Paris.

Virginia has written a number of short stories, and takes part in a regular online writing community, #Friday Flash online. She is currently working on a novel, "Echo Hall" and blogs at "A Room of My Own" (http://giniamoffatt.blogspot.com/).


**Ke Huang** As a Portuguese of Chinese descent, Ke Huang learned most of her English from watching Hollywood movies. She has a B.S. from Syracuse and M.F.A. in screenwriting from UCLA. Her writing consists of comedy, drama and horror stories about ethnic experiences.

Ke wrote "Lullaby: Barcarole" while studying for the GREs but she found that the process did not help her memorize any word. The characters in the story are inspired by Chinese-Portuguese acquaintances and friends.

**Erica Verrillo** is the author of three children's fantasy novels, *Elissa's Quest, Elissa's Odyssey* and *World's End* (Random House). She is also co-author with Lauren Gellman of a medical reference book, *Chronic Fatigue Syndrome: A Treatment Guide* (St. Martin's). Ms. Verrillo is a former resident of the State of Texas. Currently, she lives in Western Massachusetts with several imaginary friends.


**Viccy Adams** is close to finishing a PhD in creative writing at Newcastle University, where she has been researching the boundaries between short story collections and novels. Her writing has been published by – among others – Cinnamon Press, Unthank Books, Notes From The Underground, Spilling Ink Review and 4'33" magazine. Read more about her writing at www.vsadams.co.uk


**Simon Kellow-Bingham** I have spent many years working in construction management in the UK, right now I am involved in the Airports Sector. All of my most recent writing has been inspired by the strange world of the airport. Everything I write about has roots in the truth and from those roots fiction grows. My three children are my bags of gold; my wife is keeper of my heart. My words have been published in old-fashioned paper magazines and, more recently, at the OMSCWP site. I am pleased to have made the company of the other fine writers in this collection. One day I might even finish editing my untitled masterpiece.

**Paul G. Duke** lives and writes in Vancouver, on the west coast of Canada. After juggling parallel careers as a Private Investigator and Caterer to the film industry, Paul enrolled in the University of British Columbia to find answers to the metaphysical questions life had posed him, and discovered that writing fiction was the best way to explore them. When not writing, he's either in Japan with his wife, dining out in Vancouver, or sitting at home reading Dostoyevsky while watching NFL football games. In addition to putting the final polish on his first novel *Do Nothing 'til you Hear From Me*, Paul is continuing to write short stories. *Dancefloor in Outer Space* is Paul's first short fiction to be published.


**Vivienne McCulloch** To me, the short story is a little piece of magic. From the Brothers Grimm to Raymond Carver, Annie Proulx and a legion of others, the short story has never let me down. A few years ago I started writing them. I do it as often and as well as I can. I will write something longer soon, but it won't stop me from writing short stories before, during and after. I've my mother to thank for the love of reading and my partner for the gift of time to write. I live close to my birthplace in the South-West of England. I don't have any cats, but I would like a small dog at some point. Anyway, enough of me. I thank you for your time. If you would like to talk to me try @redrosevivi on Twitter.

**Ed Wood** I started writing for pleasure in my teens, short-stories mainly that imitated the type of books that I was reading at the time: Science Fiction, Fantasy, Swords and Sorcery etc. Michael Moorcock's Elric series was a particular favorite.

Recently (2010), I graduated from Exeter University with an MA in Creative Writing and I am currently working on a Crime Thriller which I hope to submit for the CWA Debut Dagger award.

I live in Plymouth and I am 40 years of age (is that middle-aged these days?). I was born in Derbyshire and have a particular love of the great outdoors, particularly The Peak District, Brecon Beacons and Dartmoor.


**Joe Miller** (pseudonym), award-winning journalist, writer, volunteer worker, has had fiction published in *Six Sentences, Ygdrasil, Flashshot* and *OMSCWP*. Has also had a few 'Bestsellers' on *YWO (Youwriteon)*, both on his own account and, with collaborator, James Natto, on their *'Births, Marriages and Deaths'* series of ultra-short, short stories.

Pieces of writing that have particularly affected me – by way of example only: Mary Oliver's poem, *'The Journey'*; Inga Clendinnen's memoir, *'Tiger's Eye'*; James Kennaway's novella, *'Silence.'*

An interesting fact about myself – on the one and only occasion went deep-sea fishing, caught a Blue Marlin. Relax. Tagged and released. (Kept all the Wahoo and the 70lb Yellowfin Tuna, though.)

The best piece of advice I've ever been offered? – Don't look down.

**John Rachel** has a B. A. in Philosophy, has travelled extensively, is a songwriter and music producer, and a left-of-left liberal. Prompted by the trauma of graduating high school and having to leave his beloved city of Detroit to attend university, the development of his social skills and world view were arrested at about age eighteen. This affliction figures prominently in all of his creative work. He is author of two full-length novels, *From Thailand With Love* and *The Man Who Loved Too Much*. He is currently living in Vietnam, while he writes his next two novels, respectively *11-11-11* and *12-12-12*.

**Abi Wyatt** writes for her life in the shadow of Carne Brea in Cornwall. Formerly a teacher of English, she was paroled in 2004 when decided to devote her time to developing her own writing. Since then, her poetry and short fiction have been widely published, both at home and abroad, and she has also become the house reviewer for Palores Press in Redruth. Abi's poetry collection, 'Moths in a Jar', (October, 2010) is available from Palores. She is now working on a new collection inspired by her interest in Saxon women.

**C.B. Heinemann**, a native of Maryland, began his musical career at the age of twelve, when he began playing with local jazz and rock bands. Later, inspired by traditional Irish groups like DeDannan, he played with master musicians and became one of

America's leading Celtic bouzouki players, performing, recording and touring throughout the United States and Europe for nearly twenty years. His Celtic rock band, Dogs Among the Bushes, was the first American Celtic group to tour in the former East Germany and Czechoslovakia after the fall of communism. That experience inspired his (still unpublished) novel *Falling Walls*. He spent two years as a street performer in Europe, and those experiences inspired a (still unpublished) literary novel, *The Last Buskers of Summer*.

    A graduate of the University of Maryland, C.B. Heinemann has written short stories for *Storyteller, Whistling Fire, Kaleidoskop,* and *Fate*. Heinemann has written travel articles for *The Washington Post, Boston Globe, Philadelphia Inquirer, Cool Traveller, Pittsburgh Post-Gazette, Car & Travel, Big World Travel,* and *Travel Reporter*.

**Clare Glennon** is delighted to be included in the second OMSCWP Anthology and is hoping that it will encourage her to do less thinking and talking about writing and more actual writing.

## Muhammad Ashfaq's "The Iron Plank"

*"It is awesome and captivating. The strength of the story comes from the myth of shab-e-Kadar and the Iranian folk-lore woven around it (Alah Rakhi and Lal Din), and its symbolic description in modern diction."*

*"A gripping round up of chilling rites. I don't agree with an earlier commenter that it is an Iranian story. Isn't it patently a Syrian one? It is a terrifying tale, which develops its own locale, law, lingo, lore, and lusts, and the reader is lost in the world of the story itself."*

*"It took me quite a while to understand the story, but when I did, it took me another quite a while to unfurl and peel off its layers. Ashfaq has craftily juxtaposed the Muslim religious fable and sub-fables within the political systems as prevalent in much of the Muslim world. Kudos to you as well for understanding a fiction replete with allusions not easily understandable in the Western World. God bless you for making this story available to us."*

All of the authors can be contacted via our website at www.millionstories.net

Alternatively you may e-mail us at the Editor@millionstories.net

Get Reading! Get Inspired! Get Writing!

The One Million Stories Creative Writing Project.